A Candlelight Ecstasy Romance®

HE LEANED FORWARD, HIS EYES FIERY WITH HUNGER . . .

She lay back with delicious acquiescence as his lips found hers. The touch of his warm lips was like fire, liquefying her with a heated desire that sent a simmering path of need through her. He was the man she had wanted, the man she had dreamed of, his lips craving hers, his body warm with urgent need, and it was real—not a fantasy, not a dream.

"Leave with me now," he breathed, his hard male frame echoing his words.

He raised his head then, and she looked into his eyes, and the desire she saw there aroused her like a physical touch.

CANDLELIGHT ECSTASY ROMANCES ®

LOVE ON ANY TERMS

Nell Kincaid

A CANDLELIGHT ECSTASY ROMANCE®

Published by
Dell Publishing Co., Inc.
1 Dag Hammarskjold Plaza
New York, New York 10017

ISBN: 0-440-11927-8

Printed in the United States of America

First printing—March 1983

To Our Readers:

We have been delighted with your enthusiastic response to Candlelight Ecstasy Romances®, and we thank you for the interest you have shown in this exciting series.

In the upcoming months we will continue to present the distinctive, sensuous love stories you have come to expect only from Ecstasy. We look forward to bringing you many more books from your favorite authors and also the very finest work from new authors of contemporary romantic fiction.

As always, we are striving to present the unique absorbing love stories that you enjoy most—books that are more than ordinary romance.

Your suggestions and comments are always welcome. Please write to us at the address below.

Sincerely,

The Editors
Candlelight Romances
1 Dag Hammarskjold Plaza
New York, New York
10017

Jennifer Preston stepped up to the stage and sat down at the table where her place card and a microphone were waiting. She was looking forward to the day's program, for she had finally learned to enjoy speaking in front of groups after years of stage fright. The audience, seated around large, flower-bedecked tables, was made up of mostly familiar faces—the beauty editors who had been covering the cosmetics field for years, along with members of the cosmetics industry itself—mostly assistants—who were there to learn and make contacts, and, of course, there were the ever-present members of the press—mostly trade journals—there to take notes and pictures of the annual cosmetics conference sponsored by *Beauty Lifestyles* magazine, hoping, naturally, for a few items of gossip as well.

Everyone in the audience was dressed well in clothes Jennifer had seen recently in *Mademoiselle,*

Glamour, and, in a few cases, *Vogue.* Jennifer dressed a bit more classically than did most of the editors. Years ago, when she had been an assistant with almost no money to spend on a wardrobe she had begun buying clothes that would look good from year to year. Now, though Jennifer was well-off financially, she had so little time to shop that she was glad she had kept to simple, classic styles. She was wearing a steel-gray silk blouse and black gabardine skirt that complemented her light-gray eyes and straight black hair, and medium-height black pumps that were, miraculously, comfortable as well as pretty.

She smiled as Helena Cairns, editor-in-chief of *Beauty Lifestyles* magazine and organizer of the conference, stepped up to the stage and picked up one of the microphones. Helena had been running these conferences, called "Beauty Issues and Answers, Hazards and Breakthroughs," for as long as anyone could remember, but she looked at least fifteen years younger than her fifty years. Jennifer cynically observed to herself that Helena's youthful appearance was probably due more to furtive visits to the plastic surgeon than to the wonders of cosmetics, but then thought perhaps not; for she herself had changed her appearance quite a bit over the past several years with nothing more than new hairstyles, different makeup, and the addition of a few pounds here and there.

"Ladies—" Helena paused, and smiled. "And I think I see a few gentlemen today as well. We'll be starting a bit late today. Alan Kelling of Eton Cosmetics won't be coming." She held up a hand to quell the audience's murmuring. "But we'll still have a full panel, and, I'm glad to say, the new president of Eton, Joseph Brennan, will also be joining us." She smiled. "He should be here any minute, but please help yourselves to cocktails in the meantime, compliments of *Beauty Lifestyles.*"

Jennifer swallowed nervously and glanced at her two colleagues on the dais. Each woman was simply reading through her notes, apparently having no great reaction to news of the switch. But neither one had been fired six years ago by Joseph Brennan, a man who had fired eight young women without even knowing what they looked like or who they were.

Jennifer stood up and made her way to the crowded bar area on the other side of the room. The idea of a Scotch and soda was suddenly very appealing; soon she'd have to get back onstage and speak to approximately fifty people with Joe Brennan not less than ten feet from where she sat, and perhaps there was a chance the drink would relax her. Better yet, maybe it would help her remember the speech, most of which had just flown from her mind. She ordered the drink and sipped it at the bar, smiling and waving perfunctorily to the editors she knew. But she wasn't comfortable simply standing around and waiting: every cell in her body suddenly felt alive with tension.

With drink in hand Jennifer threaded her way through the crowd and out into the beige-carpeted hallway; at least it was quiet out here, and she'd have a moment to relax her jangled nerves.

She walked down the hall to the elevator area, where there was a display board announcing the day's conference. On a small table nearby there was a pile of programs, and Jennifer put down her drink and picked up a few of the programs to take with her. Her father, back home in North Dakota, was still pleased to receive anything and everything that had her name or any indication of her success on it, however small, and she knew he'd like the program to show to some of his friends.

Jennifer smiled. She *had* succeeded, despite Joe Brennan's decision of six years ago, which had nearly brought a halt to her just-begun cosmetics career. She had vowed revenge then, but now she looked back on her impassioned promise-of-revenge speech to him as an impetuous act of a child long since grown up. Yes, she still resented him for what he had done, but she had done quite well for herself in any case—in spite of Joe Brennan's arrogant disregard for her and her talents.

Feeling a bit better, and certainly more relaxed, Jennifer finished her drink, gathered up a few more programs, and turned to go back to the Sky Garden.

Suddenly the elevator doors opened.

There stood Joe Brennan, his pale blue eyes as intense as ever, his wavy light brown hair a bit shorter and tinged with gray.

His eyes met hers with an impact she had forgotten: she had forgotten that deep, deep blue that beckoned, drew her into their depths; she had forgotten those heavy lids that promised the passion she had wanted so much to know.

Her lips parted and she stared, wondering whether he remembered her.

As he stepped out of the elevator he took in her

10

charcoal eyes, the jet-black hair which had once, back then, been wavy, the voluptuous figure, formerly slim.

"Which way to the Sky Garden?" he demanded.

"Uh, it's that way," Jennifer said. "Down there and to your right."

He held out a hand and she looked up sharply. What was he doing?

"I'll take one of those," he commanded impatiently, gesturing at the programs she found were still in her hand.

"Oh. Yes, here," she murmured vaguely, handing him one as she realized he thought she was an usher or hotel aide. So he didn't remember her.

"Thank you," he said curtly. "And I take it there's ice water on the podium?"

"What? Oh, yes," Jennifer answered.

"Thank you," he said in a voice that conveyed no sign of recognition, no awareness of a shared past. And he turned and strode off down the hall, his large frame moving easily and with a grace and confidence Jennifer remembered well. There was a slight but perceptible change in his physique, though, and Jennifer saw that his body had filled out in the shoulders and narrowed at the hips. His face, too, had changed in small ways: It was a bit older-looking, his jaw a bit harder, and his cheeks a bit thinner, but his eyes were the same, as easily changing as ever—at one moment pale and cold, at the next dark and hypnotic. But he still had that beautiful coloring, tanned skin with golden-brown hair than had been the object of both adoration and disdain back at Essences, Ltd. A few of the secretaries working under him had

11

started to call him—admiringly, but behind his back
—golden boy, but the description gradually became
one used more often in sarcasm and anger than admiration, for Joe Brennan was a man hated by as many
as liked him.

Without thinking Jennifer picked up her glass to
sip, but found only ice, and she silently cursed herself
for being so emotional. For she felt utterly unhinged,
a swirl of feelings weakening her knees and setting
her pulse racing. For just as Joe Brennan had forgotten her, she had forgotten her anger, burying it under
layers of other emotions, all less distracting and destructive. She had forced herself to forget—to move
on—and remembering now was painful and confusing.

By the time Jennifer returned to the Sky Garden,
Joe had already seated himself on the dais. The only
empty chair—Jennifer's—was to Joe's left, and Jennifer silently wondered what his reaction would be as
she sat down next to him. Would his surprise over
her appearance on the dais—as a speaker rather than
the hotel aide he thought she was—serve to jog his
memory?

But as Jennifer slid into her seat Joe merely turned
and smiled, shining his deep azure eyes at her in a
way that washed away—for a moment—all her anger, all her resentment from the past.

Jennifer turned away and faced the audience, annoyed over how she had weakened under Joe's gaze.
She sighed and tried to listen to Helena's welcoming
speech, but all she could do was remember. . . .

Six years earlier, Jennifer had been working at

12

Essences, Ltd., first as a summer floater, typing and doing secretarial duties wherever she was needed in the company, and then as a marketing assistant in the new-products division. She had been one of eight assistants and secretaries in a large department made up of executives, scientists, technicians, market analysts, and clerical workers, and though the work itself wasn't particularly stimulating, Jennifer had loved the atmosphere. She had been thrilled that she had found a job at her first choice of all cosmetics companies. Most of all she had been thrilled to work under a man named Joseph Brennan, of whom she had read for years in the trade papers as well as *The New York Times* and occasionally in the society columns covering charity balls and industry get-togethers.

Everyone at Essences had strong feelings about working under Joe—for he was unpredictable, ruthless, arrogant, and often rude, yet also extremely talented, a true maverick in the field, ready to listen to any suggestion, and undeniably handsome. In the few short months Jennifer had worked in his division she had been infused with what was called Brennan fever—an obsession with work, with the company, with the whole field of cosmetics. And she had found the perfect job, one in which she could grow, at a company she wanted to grow with. And now that she had also found someone whose ideas meshed with her own so well, her job seemed perfect as a jumping-off point for a promising future.

Now, as she looked back on those months and on the eager young woman who had worked so hard, the memory was edged with embarrassment: she had

13

been so young then, so naive. And now, too, as she remembered dreaming of being in Joe Brennan's arms, of making love with him, and having him need her and want her so much he'd whisper her name even in his sleep, she smiled at the memory. This fantasy, too, was one that could have been imagined only by someone much, much younger than she was now.

Yet, back then, along with countless other young women at Essences, Jennifer had let her hopes and wishes bloom as each day passed. Although she was no raving beauty, she knew she could be attractive enough when she tried. Her gray eyes and wavy black hair together with smooth, pale skin and a slim figure could look ordinary or pretty, depending on her mood and her dress, and she worked hard at looking good every day of the six months she worked at Essences.

Her fantasies grew as little events occurred. One day, at the beginning, Joe smiled at her as he passed her desk, his blue eyes sparkling with pleasure, his long, easy stride slowing as he passed. On another afternoon he held the elevator door for her in the lobby, and they rode up together, alone, and somehow she had managed to chatter away about business for the entire thirty-six-floor ride. Though later on she had no idea what she had said, she remembered well that Joe had listened attentively, even smiling broadly at one point, reacting with the easy grace that imbued everything he did.

On another day, when Jennifer was sitting at her desk at eight forty-five—which she had begun to do in the hopes that Joe would notice her—he had come striding through the secretarial area and then stopped at her desk. Jennifer had turned scarlet as she let her glance travel up from Joe's strong, hard thighs to his narrow hips, to his bulky shoulders, and finally, his glinting blue eyes, and lips curved in amused pleasure. He had winked at her, pursed his lips, and let his gaze rove over her. "Just what I like to see," he said, and walked away as quickly as he had come. Jennifer spent the rest of the morning trying to figure out whether he had been referring to her looks or the fact that she was there early, reluctantly concluding it was probably the latter.

Yet her adulation and attraction had lasted, with little bits of encouragement from Joe here and there. One day, after she had been working as an assistant for a few weeks, her supervisor asked her to work late, filling in for Mr. Brennan's assistant. Jennifer felt elated and pleasantly panicky, but annoyed as well. For she hadn't looked worse in weeks, and was wearing her least attractive outfit. Lately she had begun to feel there was no point in trying to make herself look good: she was noticed infrequently, and it was demoralizing to see other young women, who were better paid, coming in to work with consistently nicer outfits. Well, Joe probably wouldn't notice her anyway, she reasoned, so what did it really matter?

But the evening had been wonderful nevertheless, more than she had let herself imagine it would be. Joe had asked her to analyze the past performances of various print media, mostly magazines, in an ad campaign that had run a few months before. It was a job that was normally done by Joe's assistant or by media planners in Jennifer's department, but there was a board meeting in two days, and Joe wanted the information right away. As he explained the work to her, Jennifer was filled with confidence and pleasure. She had done this sort of work before, and knew she could do it well and quickly.

"This may take more than one night of overtime, Jen," he said softly, looking down at her from where he was sitting on the desk. She loved hearing him say "Jen," a nickname she usually hated when strangers used it. But Joe had said it as if he knew her well, and as if he liked her. "And if you can set aside tomorrow," he said, "and perhaps tomorrow evening, if you're not busy, we could wrap it up."

She smiled, hardly believing her ears. "I'm not busy," she said dreamily.

He patted her hand and stood up. "Great," he said. "And order two of whatever you want for dinner, all right? Come and get me in my office whenever you're ready, and we can eat out here. I'll look over what you've done."

After he left, Jennifer could hardly work the electric pencil sharpener, much less perform a complex analysis. She sat at her desk with paper, computer printouts, a calculator, and ten sharpened pencils in front of her, remembering Joe's words and glances over and over and over. And remembering his touch, casual but perhaps meaningful. Somehow, though, she realized the evening would not be the idyll she was fantasizing if she kept sitting and dreaming, so she set to work furiously. By the time she ordered dinner—roast beef sandwiches, soda, and coffee— she was half-finished with her task, and wished she had worked more slowly so her time with Joe would be longer. But she knew that was silly. She was here to work, not to . . . whatever.

A bit later, over dinner, Joe looked at Jennifer in amazement when he saw how much she had done. "This is fantastic," he said. "At this rate you can knock off in an hour and be finished before lunch if you work on it tomorrow morning."

"Well, I don't know about that," she said. "Maybe the second part will go more slowly."

Joe laughed. "Modesty is a very nice quality, Jen. But don't use it at work, all right? It won't take you far." He gazed into her eyes. "And you will go far, you know."

For a moment they looked into each other's eyes wordlessly.

Joe smiled. "Well," he said brightly, "back to the salt mines. Just let me know when you're leaving, Jen, and I'll call you a cab."

"That's okay," she said. "I know how to get a taxi." And then she silently cursed herself: *he* knew she knew how to get a cab; that wasn't the point.

He winked. "Whatever you say. I'll see you in the morning then."

Somehow the next morning the spell was gone. Joe was businesslike and almost brusque, and when Jennifer finished the report at noon, he wasn't even in. She had to leave the work with his secretary. And that was that.

She continued to work hard, determined to do well with or without Joe Brennan. But in the back of her mind she also judged everything she did in terms of what Joe would think. Would he like the report she had written, or the dress she was wearing?

17

A few days after the night she had worked late with him, Jennifer saw him enter the coffee shop in the lobby. He stood by the door in a small clutch of people waiting for seats, looking a bit impatient but resigned to waiting. Jennifer, sitting at a small table, finally caught Joe's eye and waved him over. And despite her vague fears that Joe wouldn't want to sit at her table, or that he wouldn't even recognize her out of context, he seemed delighted at her invitation to share the table. Jennifer felt horribly self-conscious as he watched her eat while he waited for his food. Her club sandwich suddenly seemed a mile high and infuriatingly difficult to eat. But she managed, and soon forgot her fears as they talked easily and enthusiastically about work. He didn't gaze at her as he had at the office, but perhaps, she thought hopefully, he was more reserved in public places.

Toward the end of the meal he asked if she usually ate lunch alone.

Jennifer shrugged uncomfortably. She had always spent much time alone, and had been made keenly aware of it by her parents and friends. "I—sometimes," she said, then smiled. "Usually. I don't have that many friends at the office."

He searched her eyes. "You *are* a bit different, actually," he said gently. "More serious, perhaps. I've noticed that." He paused. "Among other things," he added.

She smiled.

"I've enjoyed the lunch," he said. "Now please let me pay for it."

And they walked back through the lobby together,

18

Jennifer feeling she had gone miles toward forging a relationship with Joe.

And then, two days later, it was all over, quite suddenly.

That last day was etched in Jennifer's memory as clearly as if it had happened only yesterday. She had been summoned to see Mrs. Hollins, the office manager and, not knowing what to expect but assuming it was good news, sat down and smiled expectantly as Mrs. Hollins seated herself behind her desk.

Mrs. Hollins calmly explained that there had been a serious information leak in Jennifer's department. Someone had revealed the name of the new lipstick-and-nail-polish line, a name which had been invented by Joe Brennan and which hadn't even been revealed to the advertising agency yet. And the name had turned up at one of their rival companies.

Mrs. Hollins looked into Jennifer's eyes. "We're asking each young woman in the department, Jennifer, whether she knows anything about that leak. Now I'm asking you." She brushed back a strand of gray hair and waited.

Jennifer widened her eyes and met Mrs. Hollins's gaze. "I don't know anything about it, Mrs. Hollins," she said honestly. Yet she felt so self-conscious, she was certain she looked as if she were lying. Her cheeks were flaming, and she suspected, too, that her gaze had perhaps been too direct. But there was nothing she could do.

As Mrs. Hollins had said, they did interview each of the typists and assistants in the department. The atmosphere in the clerical area grew increasingly

19

tense and quiet as the day wore on and each young woman was called out of the room.

At the end of the day Mrs. Hollins came in and called for everyone's attention. She looked older somehow, her lips set in grim tension as her glance swept the room. "I'll come right to the point," she said. "We've asked each of you the same question." She sighed. "I'm both pleased and sorry to say we had no reason to suspect any one person in the department." She looked at each of the young women, all sitting in rapt attention. "Unfortunately," she said slowly, "we're going to have to let all of you go."

The rest of her words Jennifer heard yet hardly took in: that they would each be "laid off due to reorganization," that they would receive "fine" recommendations plus two weeks' pay. And finally that they would not be "permitted on the premises of the company after five p.m. that day," all by order of Joe Brennan.

Jennifer sat at her desk in shock as several of the young women rushed up to Mrs. Hollins, calling out anxious questions and begging her to reconsider. She hardly heard the steady staccato of questions, hardly heard the voices or saw those worried faces. For Mrs. Hollins's words kept coming back: "by order of Joe Brennan."

And Jennifer hated him, hated this man for whom she would have done almost anything, this man for whom she had run herself ragged these past months, this man of whom she had dreamed so many times.

And then the full realization of what had happened hit her. Beyond Joe Brennan's cold betrayal, which was something she would perhaps learn to live with though never forget, the hard fact remained that she was out of a job. Out of work. Unemployed, without warning, and without reason. By order of Joe Brennan.

For as long as she could remember, she had planned to have a career. Back home, when friends of hers had gotten married right after high school, part of her had envied them. She had never been seriously involved with any of the boys she knew. Yet, in going to college and planning a career, she had known she was taking the right steps—right for her if not for her friends. After college she had come all the way to New York and found a job in the industry she had dreamed of. Though it wasn't the greatest job in the world, it was a start, and an excellent one. And it had just been ripped from her grasp.

Her heart raced as she thought of writing to her father back home. There was no way to let him know she had lost her job without upsetting him deeply. Yet she didn't want to keep the news from him; though she saw him only once a year, she wrote to him often—more so since her mother had died—and she had told him many times about Essences and her plans for her future at the company. Now she would have to explain this disastrous, unexpected setback. By order of Joe Brennan.

And suddenly she knew what she would do. She would talk to Joe, face-to-face. He had seen her working hard all these months; he had said he liked her; he had said she'd "go far"; and she had a rapport with him that he didn't seem to have with the other assistants. True, it wasn't the relationship she spent so much of her time fantasizing about, but it was a relationship nevertheless. That day at lunch he had even given her reason to believe that he did think of her in a special way.

Perhaps when she spoke with him, reasoned with him, he would change his mind. It was certainly worth a try in any case.

And thus, while the seven other women in the department crowded around Mrs. Hollins, Jennifer quietly left the room and walked down to the end of the hall to the large wooden door marked JOSEPH BRENNAN in clean brass lettering.

His secretary, Jackie, wasn't at her desk, so Jennifer knocked on Joe's door herself, tentatively and then loudly, as she silently repeated her resolve: Joe would listen to her. She would talk, and he would listen, and she would get her job back.

"Come in," growled an angry male voice.

When Jennifer opened the door Joe didn't look up from whatever he was writing. His wavy hair hung down over his forehead as he leaned over his desk, and his large shoulders were straining against the fabric of his white shirt.

Jennifer felt a wave of sadness wash over her as she looked at him. She had wanted those arms around her so many times; now she was here to fight. She had wanted those eyes to shine into hers, those lips to brush against her own, that voice to whisper softly in her ear. And the man wasn't even looking at her.

"Yes?" he demanded, again without looking up.

And Jennifer was suddenly angry. Who did he think he was, not even looking up when someone came into his office? Strengthened by anger, she strode up to his desk with confidence.

Without putting his pen down he glanced up at Jennifer and then went back to writing. "Where the hell is Jackie?" he asked irritably. "Whatever you have for me, leave out there with my secretary, please."

"I don't 'have' anything for you, Mr. Brennan," she said steadily.

The pen stopped. Joe Brennan dropped it and looked up at Jennifer, his eyes cold and pale and unquestioning. "What did you say?" he asked coolly.

She met his ice-blue eyes with resolute directness. "I said, Mr. Brennan, that I don't have anything for you. I'm here to speak with you, not to drop something off with your secretary."

He looked at her assessingly, his eyes roving from her face down her voluptuous figure back to her flashing gray eyes. "I don't recall having an appointment at this hour. What's—"

"I don't have an appointment," Jennifer interrupted. "But it's important that I speak with you," she added more softly, realizing he would probably be more receptive if she were a bit less aggressive.

His eyes swept over her figure. "Well," he said slowly, exhaling in resignation, "I'll give you three minutes." He looked at his watch and then into her eyes with challenge.

"All right," Jennifer snapped. "I want you to make an exception with me, Mr. Brennan. I've worked my heart out for this job—coming in early, staying late, everything. You know I wasn't responsible for that leak. You must know that, and . . ."

Her voice trailed off as he put his head in his

23

hands. When he looked up at her his eyes were less cold, less challenging. "I hadn't realized," he said softly, "that you were one of those."

Jennifer stared. "One of those?" she asked numbly. "Is that how you think of all of us, as 'those'?" And worse yet, was that how he thought of *her,* as just one of a group of faceless, nameless young women?

He sighed. "Look, Jennifer. I'm really sorry. I just didn't know. . . . I didn't sit down and think of who was involved." He sighed. "But there's really nothing I can do." He leaned back and set his palms on the desk. "I just don't think it would be fair to make an exception. What about the other innocent young women? What would I say to them? So, I'm sorry, as I said, but you should have no trouble getting another job. You're more than capable." He raised a brow. "And though I know this isn't supposed to enter into it—and you'll probably brand me a male chauvinist forever—I must say your being as easy on the eyes as you are won't hurt."

Jennifer ignored his appreciative gaze. "In other words," she said quietly, trying to keep her voice steady, "you won't reconsider."

He shook his head. "I'm sorry, Jennifer. I just can't do that." He pursed his lips. "I realize this may sound patronizing," he said slowly, sitting forward, "and I don't blame you for being upset, but you may thank me someday. This may be just what you needed to set you on your way."

Her eyes widened. "Oh, please," she said sarcastically. "Spare me that speech." She shook her head. "I have friends who've gotten the same spiel from their bosses, and believe me, it's just something executives say so they can pat themselves on the back and assuage their guilt." She raised a brow. "But let me tell you something, Joe Brennan. I think what you did today is rotten. Seven—or maybe eight—completely innocent young woman have lost their jobs unnecessarily." She inhaled deeply. "And I'll never forget that. Or forgive you for that. And one day you'll come to me and ask me for some sort of professional favor—as I came to you today." She turned and walked to the door, then opened it and faced him. "And when you do," she breathed, "I'll pay you back a thousand times over for what you did today." And she walked quickly down the hall before he could reply.

When she got home that night the pressures and tensions of the afternoon burst forth, and she cried angry and bitter tears, wondering how she could have been so naive, so foolish, so disconnected from reality. For six months she had analyzed Joe Brennan's every action, guessed at and hoped for hidden meanings in every glance of his, every word he had spoken, however casually. And he hadn't cared one bit about her.

The anger that had been born that day carried Jennifer through a grueling job search that had taken two months but felt like a year. She worked as a waitress at night so she would have time to schedule interviews during the day, and finally found and accepted a public-relations-assistant position at Civette Scents, Inc., a small but growing company. And then she had worked hard, becoming a marketing assistant, assistant marketing manager, and then, a month ago, marketing director, when her boss left. She had taken marketing, copywriting, and graphics arts courses at night, and spent almost every evening either in class or at work. In all that time she had nearly gone off track only once, when she had become involved with a man at Civette, and, when things got unpleasant, thought she'd have to leave the company. Luckily he had left, and she had kept her job. And over the years she had thought she had come far enough to forget that awful day six years earlier with Joe Brennan.

Yet now, years later, sitting next to Joe Brennan as a colleague rather than an underling, she was surprised at how vividly she remembered her years-old anger.

-TWO-

As Jennifer's turn to speak approached, she was suddenly as nervous as if she were speaking in front of a group for the first time. Joe's presence next to her felt like a dare of sorts, a challenge that she do her best to show him how good she was.

Yet by the time she was two minutes into her speech on perfume marketing, she knew the dare had done more good than harm. Reporters from the trade journals were taking rapid and copious notes, and their photographers were snapping her picture. When she finished, the applause was loud and long. She was pleased, and she smiled, but her mind wasn't on the reporters or the audience. She couldn't help it, but she was wondering what Joe had thought of her speech. She wanted him to remember her and see how far she had come over the years. Annoyed with herself for feeling so vulnerable to this man sitting next to her, Jennifer concentrated on fielding the questions members of the audience asked.

And then it was Joe's turn to speak. As he spoke he held the audience in rapt and delighted attention; when they laughed, it was as if on cue, and when they listened it was with utter absorption.

Jennifer was intrigued and annoyed. He hadn't lost his touch.

But the conference was over before Jennifer knew, and she was suddenly confronted with a new quandary. Now that she had met Joe Brennan after all these years, was she going to say or do anything about his past actions? Of course, she didn't necessarily have to make a choice at the moment; she now shared with him a vast professional arena in which she would no doubt have much to do with him in the future. But was there anything to be said or done now?

Joe answered her question himself as he stood up and turned to her, his dark blue eyes melting into hers, holding her in a gaze she couldn't break. "I hadn't realized," he murmured softly, "until you began to speak." His lips curled in pleasure. "Your voice hasn't changed a bit, Jennifer. I can hear you vowing revenge on me even now."

She inhaled deeply and tore her gaze from his, but when she found herself looking at his broad chest and his handsome frame, she decided perhaps his eyes were safer after all. "That was a long time ago," she said, embarrassed that he apparently remembered the speech so well. She had been young and naive back then . . . though her anger had lasted.

"Then I'd say we had a lot of catching up to do," he said quietly. "I've missed a lot being in California these past three years, but I've followed your progress in the trades." He tilted his head. "I knew you'd go far."

She turned from him and began gathering up her papers. "You knew no such thing," she said, her voice low and controlled. "But there's hardly much point in rehashing the whole thing now." She snapped her briefcase shut, intending to leave without any further conversation. If she were going to have anything to do with Joe Brennan in the future, she would have to be calmer than she was at the moment. She simply couldn't think straight while he was standing so close, while his voice tugged at her with a strength greater than her resolves.

"How about a lift, then, back to your office?" he asked. "I have a limo outside."

She gave him a cold smile. "I don't think so. It's a beautiful day and I'd rather walk."

A glimmer of a smile played on his lips. "Then I'll walk too. Eton's only a block from Civette anyway."

Jennifer shrugged. "Suit yourself," she said, enjoying the fact that after all these years he was now—if in only a minor way—pursuing her.

Once they were out on the street in the spring air and Joe had sent his car and driver back to the office, Jennifer felt a rush of happiness, despite the company she shared. The tulips had bloomed on the nearby swells of grass in the park, and Central Park South had at least half a dozen flower-bedecked horses and carriages trotting along into the park. The day was lovely enough to make Jennifer forget her old anger, to set it aside and simply enjoy a beautiful springtime

29

walk downtown with an attractive if slightly annoying man.

"Well," he said, taking her arm as they walked past the Plaza Hotel and began to head downtown. "In a sense we both have new jobs to celebrate, Jennifer. You've been marketing director at Civette what—a month?"

"Mmm," she said vaguely, trying to ignore the warmth emanating from Joe's closeness. He was much taller than she, but she had always had a good stride, and they walked easily together, as if they had been doing so for a long time.

"And do you like it?" he asked.

She looked up at him. There was something in his tone she couldn't read. "Yes, of course," she answered, and then added, "much more than I did Essences."

He raised a brow. "I thought we weren't going to discuss all of that," he said.

She sighed. "Yes. Well . . ." Her voice trailed off. She didn't want to discuss the past, and he was respecting her wishes. She was the one who couldn't stop thinking about it. "Well, anyway," she said brightly, forcing herself to another subject, "business really has been great—and this year should be our best yet, I think."

"Mmm," he answered distractedly.

As she realized Joe wasn't listening, unbidden memories returned. She remembered when Joe hadn't listened to her six years ago, when she had been so wrong about what their relationship was. And she was falling into the trap once again, assuming he was involved when in fact he was somewhere else entirely. She was about to break away from his grasp when he spoke.

"Look, Jennifer. I went to the conference for a special reason—not just to speak." He looked at his watch, the same gold Rolex, Jennifer noticed, that he had worn back at Essences, and then at Jennifer. "It's only four o'clock. Why don't you come along to my office for a moment? I want to talk to you."

She tried to steel herself against the languorous pull of his voice. "About what?" she asked coolly.

He pursed his lips, barely suppressing a smile. "I can see we're going to have to settle that old business," he mused. "But we can talk about it another time. What I want to do, quite simply, is steal you from Civette. My marketing director left last week. And you'd be absolutely perfect."

Jennifer halted involuntarily in her tracks, and her arm fell out of Joe's grasp. "I . . . don't think so," she said carefully, annoyed she had reacted so strongly—and physically—to his words. It was completely unprofessional.

His gaze was direct. "Why not? Why not consider it at least?"

"Because," she answered, measuring every word, "I'm quite happy where I am, Joe, and my experience with you has been . . . well, it's not something I'd like to repeat."

He cocked a brow. "Aren't you making a rather hasty decision? You don't even know the position I'm offering. And you haven't even seen our offices— what could be your office, and your staff. Just come and have a look, and a drink, at least."

Jennifer smiled inwardly as she considered his

31

proposition. Here was Joe Brennan, the man she had adored and then hated, asking her to work with him just as she had wished for six years ago, looking at her in a way she had dreamed of six years ago, and she could say no. She *would* say no, of course. She had learned enough about Joe Brennan and his corporate style on that one day back then to keep herself away from him for a lifetime. And so, she told herself, it didn't really matter if she explored his proposal, did it? She had the upper hand to an extent she wouldn't have imagined possible six years ago, and she was going to draw out the pleasure as long as she could. "I'll come," she said, "but just to look around."

His eyes sparkled with confident pleasure. "That's all I ask," he said, and as Jennifer fell in beside him once again, she tried to shake the feeling that she had just fallen into some sort of trap.

And a clever trap it was, Jennifer thought later, for, despite her resolve that the tour of the Eton offices would be purely exploratory, Jennifer couldn't help imagining herself as part of the Eton staff almost immediately. From the sleek modern reception area—unusual because it afforded a spectacular view of Central Park and Manhattan's Upper East Side—to Joe's own office, quietly elegant with low, modern furniture and muted grays—it had the look of a place in which serious business was undertaken, but with an enthusiasm and verve missing in many offices. On all the walls there were blown-up posters of the company's most recent ads—including their latest, for a series of men's colognes and products called, simply, Eton.

Joe showed Jennifer one of the research and development labs at the end of a corridor, explaining that they did most of their R&D work in New Jersey. And then he led her back to his office, which had a much-larger-than-life-size poster of their latest ad for their new perfume, Ardence—a beautiful young woman with waist-length, flaming red hair in the arms of a dark and very lusty-looking pirate.

Joe seated himself on the gray leather couch half-facing the poster, and Jennifer sat down next to him. He glanced up at the poster and then at Jennifer. "Like it?" he asked confidently.

Jennifer shrugged. She had seen the ad only once —in *Cosmopolitan*—and though it was eye-catching, she didn't think it would be a successful ad campaign. "I think it's good esthetically—it's eye-catching and really nice to look at." She shook her head. "But it's a bit of yesterday's news, don't you think? I'm surprised your people put this together." She smiled inwardly as she watched him grow visibly annoyed. This was a power she had never felt before. She continued with pleasure. "A few years ago it would have been fine—fantasies of pirates and all that." She shrugged. "But that's what it looks like— a few years old."

Joe's eyes roved over her—over her hair, her eyes, her mouth—and she warmed under his scrutiny. "You certainly sound sure of yourself," he said softly.

"I am," she answered. "About that," she added quietly, and then wished she hadn't.

"And what aren't you sure of?" Joe murmured, his eyes drawing her into their oceans of azure.

"I . . ." The words left her as she was captured by his gaze, and it was as if nothing existed but those deep blue eyes.

He reached out and gently ran a finger down her neck to the hollow of her throat, which was pulsing quickly with desire. "I'm sure of one thing, Jennifer," he said quietly, his voice edged with a male need that touched her almost physically. His fingers traced a path along the edge of her blouse, inflaming her skin in their ardent quest. "I'm glad I saw you today," he said softly, his voice almost a whisper, "and I'm glad you're here now. . . ." He inhaled deeply, his gaze melting into hers with an urgency that made her breathless with desire.

He leaned forward, his eyes fiery with hunger, and she lay back with delicious acquiescence as his lips found hers. The touch of his warm lips was like fire, liquefying her with a heated, rolling desire that sent a simmering path of need through her. He was the man she had wanted, the man she had dreamed of, his lips craving hers, his body warm with urgent need, and it was real—not a fantasy, not a dream. Her lips parted and his tongue entered her mouth, coaxing, exploring, arousing her with hunger, feeding her desire with an intensity that was thrilling. Her questing fingers worked up his muscled back to his strong neck, his thick hair, and he answered with a moan of need that sent a shock of melting fire through her. He trailed his hands over her body, along her waist, over her hips, and her body trembled, aching with desire.

He tore his mouth from hers and roved a blazing damp path to her ear. "You're so lovely," he whispered, his breath hot, his voice low and urgent. "Lovelier than I had remembered," he breathed, his admiring eyes echoing his words. "I'm so glad I saw you today." His lips were close to hers, his breath warm against her mouth. And when she looked into his eyes, the desire in them aroused her like a physical touch. "We can talk later," he murmured, his eyes half-closed with passion. "I just know I want you here with me."

The words were vague, heard through layers of desire and a haze of need. But they reached her. "I—what did you say?" she whispered.

He kissed her on the neck and then looked into her eyes. "We'd be so good together. In every way. To have you here . . ."

She blinked and felt suddenly alert—and wary. Desire had been replaced with unwelcome comprehension, washing over her like slow waves on the sand. He was being purposely vague, purposely confusing. And she felt as if she were in the arms of a stranger. For she had forgotten as she had been wrapped in his arms—forgotten that he wanted something from her, forgotten that he was unendingly ambitious, forgotten that he had always known how to get what he wanted.

She had to stay away from him: her life was fine as it was. Strong as she was, she had just discovered, as perhaps she had always known, that saying no in the arms of a man whose kiss could arouse her so strongly could be very difficult indeed. No, she didn't need him, professionally or emotionally, and she didn't want him. He was an operator, used to getting what he wanted through whatever means were necessary—including charm. And she wouldn't fall for it.

"What's the matter?" he asked quietly. When she looked at him, she was surprised to see that his eyes were soft, gentle, filled with regret and confusion. But that, too, was probably something he could turn on and off at will.

"I think I've had enough of the Brennan charm for one afternoon, Joe." She stood up. "And I don't see any reason to waste your time or mine talking about a job here. I'm sure I'll see you around." She picked up her purse and strode out without looking back.

THREE

When Jennifer returned to her office that afternoon, she forced herself to forget her meeting with Joe. She had far too many things to worry about to let a chance encounter dominate her thoughts. In addition to hectic promotion problems with a new line of hair products at Civette, a second cousin, Caroline Connors, was coming to stay at her apartment for a few days.

Jennifer sighed as she looked out her window at the darkening skyscape of the city. Poor Caroline. From what Jennifer could discern over the phone, Caroline sounded even more naive than Jennifer had been at that age—full of expectations that couldn't possibly be fulfilled, hopes that could never be met. And she was no doubt destined for immediate disappointment, for she needed a job and an apartment—both nearly impossible to find quickly in New York.

Yet, in one way, Jennifer was glad Caroline was

coming, for she'd distract Jennifer from remembering those deep azure eyes she had seen that day, the warm lips that had caressed her skin with a fervor she couldn't forget.

When she arrived, Caroline was indeed a distraction, if not an entirely welcome one. She was endlessly cheerful, a curly-haired blonde who seemed not to have a care in the world, and who never, ever stopped chattering away. When she arrived at Jennifer's small but elegant apartment on Eighty-sixth and East End Avenue, she greeted Jennifer as if they were the best of friends seeing each other after a long separation, when in fact they hadn't seen each other in fifteen years. The whole apartment had suddenly been filled with her presence—her clothes, her voice, what seemed like a hundred magazines she had brought on the plane from California.

Now, as Caroline sat on one of Jennifer's two new Haitian cotton couches with classified ads spread all around her, Jennifer felt a wave of apprehension. Having Caroline stay would be difficult, and would certainly be longer than a mere "few days" unless something extraordinary happened.

Caroline shone her big brown eyes at her cousin and smiled. "I'm really excited, Jennifer. Look at this classified section from the *Times*. There must be a million jobs in here."

Jennifer smiled. "Well, don't be too disappointed, Caroline, if things don't happen for you right away, okay? You're trying to do two of the most difficult things to do in New York—find a job and an apartment. And I'd help you, but I don't know of any openings right now, except maybe through the agencies." She hoped she didn't sound too discouraging, but she wanted to prepare Caroline for what could be a very trying several months.

"I don't know," Caroline said, shrugging her shoulders. "I have a lot of experience that you didn't have when you started looking. You had just graduated from college, right?"

"Well, yes, but—"

"Well, I've had a whole year of experience. Six months as a secretary, and six months as an assistant, and I'm just going to say I was an assistant. So I'm way ahead. I'm not straight out of school." She lifted the newspaper off the couch and onto the coffee table. Where the paper had been there was now a large gray stain on the off-white fabric, and Caroline and Jennifer simultaneously looked at the stain and then at each other.

Caroline's eyes were wide and filled with emotion. "I'm sorry," she breathed. "I'm really sorry."

Jennifer sighed. Her new couch, and it already looked filthy. But her cousin looked so upset, even frightened, it would have been cruel to act angry. "Never mind," she said, in a comforting tone. "Just keep all those newspapers away from the couch from now on, all right?"

Caroline nodded quickly and stacked her papers and magazines on the table.

Jennifer went over to the bar she had set up in the large foyer and made herself a drink. Somehow she knew the next few weeks wouldn't be easy.

It was the very next evening when Caroline came

home bursting with good news. Jennifer was sitting on the couch looking over some copy she had brought home—she had thought it would be best not to work late with Caroline staying at her place—and Caroline had come running in, slammed the door, and flung herself on the couch opposite Jennifer.

"I just got a job!" she cried. "My first day in New York and I got a job!"

"That's wonderful!" Jennifer cried, smiling. "Tell me all about it."

"Oh, Jennifer, it's perfect! And we'll both be working in cosmetics! I'll be at Eton—you know, those ads where there's that couple walking through the woods, and—"

"I know," Jennifer cut in. She could hardly believe it. Eton! "I . . . tell me about the job, Caroline."

Caroline frowned. "What's the matter? Aren't you excited?"

"Yes, of course. But tell me . . . who are you working for?"

"Well, I'll be doing what I was doing in California —being an assistant in the P.R. department—which is still kind of boring at my level, but I know I can get promoted. Anyway, I was interviewed first by personnel, then by a guy named Alan Kelling, who's kind of head of the department, I think. And then by the president. Oh, and he said he knew you—what's his name?—Joseph Brennan. Joe Brennan."

Jennifer nodded. "Yes, I . . . I used to know him." She frowned. "How did I come up in the conversation though?"

Caroline shrugged. "Oh, I guess I was rambling on a little bit, and I said I was really excited even to be

40

interviewed because I had just come to New York, and how my cousin who I'm staying with worked in the same field."

"I see," Jennifer said.

"So what's bugging you?" Caroline asked. "You act as if you're not excited."

Jennifer sighed. "No, Caroline, I'm really happy for you. I'm just, well, I'm probably worrying unnecessarily, but I wish you were working anyplace other than at Eton."

Caroline frowned. "But why?"

As Jennifer told her the story of her past experiences with Joe Brennan—leaving out her early feelings for him—she was once again struck by how naive she had been back then, and how little she had understood of the world. The job she had lost because of Joe had been a minor one, and she had come far despite all that had happened. Joe's actions, as it turned out, had had little effect on her career. "Well," she finished, "I guess with jobs being so hard to come by, Caroline, you obviously have to take them up on their offer."

Caroline looked surprised. "I already did," she said. "And anyway, I'm sure I won't have anything to do with that Brennan guy. I mean, he's the president of the company, and anyway he seems like—really conceited. I'm just glad to have the job though."

Jennifer smiled. "I'm really happy for you," she said. Yet, as she stood up and went into the kitchen to start making dinner, she wondered why her voice had sounded so hollow.

* * *

Despite Caroline's initial happiness over finding the job at Eton, her enthusiasm waned almost immediately. She was bored and unhappy after she had been at the company less than a week, and she complained to Jennifer about it every night. Apparently morale at Eton was extremely low, and had not improved a bit since Joe Brennan had become president. The one good thing, Caroline said glumly as she began setting the table for dinner, was that Mr. Brennan had bought everyone tickets for the Fragrance and Cosmetics Institute's annual charity ball, and that sounded like it might be fun.

Jennifer was surprised to hear this. Tickets to the annual charity event—this year, it was to benefit a foundling home—cost one hundred dollars per person, and Joe had obviously spent a considerable sum of either his own or the company's money, no doubt to help lift everyone's spirits. It didn't fit with the image she had of him.

"Are you going?" Caroline asked as she sat down at the table.

"I . . . yes," Jennifer answered, wondering why she had even hesitated. "The company pays, and it isn't a bad place to make contacts, along with helping whatever charity it's for. Everyone from the industry is there."

"Well, maybe you can put in a good word for me with Mr. Brennan, Jennifer. Ask him to promote me or something."

Jennifer laughed. "Aren't you rushing things a bit? Anyway, he'd hardly listen to *me.*"

"Yes, he would," Caroline insisted. "Or he might. You can't tell. When we were talking about you at my interview, he said he thought you were one of the top marketing people in the industry."

Jennifer smiled inwardly. "Yes. Well. I think you'd do better on your own, Caroline. I really do." Yet, as she spoke, an image came into her mind, not her usual picture of Joe as an arrogant and brusque man, not the angry picture she had formed from her last day at Essences, but a new one, of Joe holding her in his arms as he had last week, looking into her eyes with the deep blue enveloping gaze that melted into hers, brushing her lips with his and murmuring, "Just tell me what you want, Jennifer. I want *you* . . . what is it that you want?"

A liquid warmth flowed through her as she pictured the scene so vividly that she could almost feel his strong arms around her, almost taste his coaxing tongue and ardent lips, almost inhale the male need that was so palpably clear.

She shook her head. What was she thinking? Those fantasies were over. They had ended when she had finally grown up enough to know that she had to love a man to make love with him. Yet she had to admit it was difficult to forget how swiftly she had succumbed to that kiss in Joe's office. And she also had to admit that in that one brief kiss he had awakened in her a need she had closed herself off from for a long time.

But she knew, too, that she was mature enough to keep the experience in its proper compartment of her life. It had happened, and it was over now. She would simply have to keep her physical distance from Joe in the future. He did not belong in her life. He never had, and he never would.

* * *

That Thursday afternoon, just as Jennifer was getting ready to leave her office, the phone rang. Everyone else had left, and Jennifer answered it herself on the first ring, hoping it would somehow be a wrong number. She was exhausted, and if she didn't hurry up and get home, she'd be at least an hour late to the ball, which was being held at Regine's on Park Avenue.

"Jennifer Preston," she said quietly, her voice ragged with fatigue.

"I certainly hope you're not too tired to dance tonight," said a smooth male voice, caressing her like the touch of a man's hand.

She half-hoped it was Joe, half-knew it was.

"Joe Brennan," he answered, as if reading her thoughts. "You *are* coming tonight?"

"Yes. I'm late as it is, though, so—"

"How about a lift then?" he cut in. "I'm just leaving Eton now, and my driver can take you to your place if—"

"No, thanks," she cut in. "I've got a cab waiting," she lied.

"All right," he said, "but I'll be waiting for you at Regine's." He paused. "Are you sure you won't take me up on my offer?"

A picture flashed through her mind, that same damned picture of lips against lips, breathless moans, fevered touches, and she unconsciously shook her head. "What? Oh, no, I'll see you later."

"Don't keep that cab waiting," he advised. Then he said good-bye and hung up.

Jennifer smiled and replaced the receiver. Perhaps

44

her lie had been transparent, but she wouldn't let the thought bother her. The most important priority, at the moment, was keeping her distance, even if she suffered a little embarrassment in the process.

When she arrived back at her apartment she found Caroline standing in the foyer looking at herself in the closet's full-length mirror. She looked completely different, having been transformed from a nearly chubby curly-haired girl to a voluptuous, surprisingly sophisticated-looking young woman. The long strapless crêpe de chine dress she wore looked extremely expensive, and followed the curves of her figure as only a truly well-made dress can.

Jennifer put down her purse and stared. "Well. You're certainly doing yourself up for the evening."

Caroline beamed. "It's a *ball,* Jennifer. I mean, the invitation actually says Annual Charity Ball!"

Jennifer smiled. "Well, yes, Caroline, but it isn't actually. You don't have to get quite that dressed up."

When she saw Caroline's smile begin to fade she added, "But you look fantastic, hon. Really. Where'd you get your dress?"

As Caroline turned away and knelt to fasten her sandals, Jennifer had the oddest impression that Caroline didn't want her to know. "Oh, a store that was having a sale. Over on Sixth Avenue."

"Really? What's it called? I'd like to go," Jennifer said, although it was an intention she probably wouldn't be able to carry out. She was just too busy these days to go shopping.

"Oh, I forget the name," Caroline said vaguely. "But the sale ended today anyway. You know, it was

45

one of those stores where there are three thousand hideous dresses and one nice one."

Jennifer laughed, but once again she had the feeling that Caroline was trying to hide something. And then she knew, at once, what it was. Caroline had obviously spent a lot of money on the dress and felt awkward having spent so lavishly on herself when Jennifer was providing her with a free room. Jennifer knew, too, that she'd have to talk to Caroline soon about finding an apartment of her own. But she wanted to wait, to be sure Caroline felt settled and relaxed enough to do so. If she felt pressured, she'd probably take the first apartment she saw, even if it were the size of a closet.

Jennifer left Caroline fiddling with her dress and went into the bedroom to find something to wear. All of a sudden she felt as if she had absolutely nothing that would be appropriate for the occasion; Joe's call had seen to that. If she wore something particularly attractive or sexy, she'd call attention to herself in a way she wasn't certain she wanted to. But the other option wouldn't do at all. Looking plain or too casual was just silly and would do little for her image or her fun that evening.

Jennifer finally settled on a beige silk short-sleeved sheath that buttoned down the front and was belted softly at the waist. It fit her well, flowing along the curves of her body without appearing tight, and it was comfortable yet formal enough for the evening. She was pleased with the way she looked, even when Caroline came in and sat down with her in front of the dressing-table mirror and she saw how much older she looked than her young cousin. The age

46

difference gave her confidence all of a sudden. She was glad she wasn't nineteen years old anymore, glad her gray eyes looked as if they had seen a bit of what there was to see in the world. For in Caroline she saw herself nine years earlier, and remembered how uncomfortable those times had been.

And once again she was struck by how much stronger she was now than she had been then. Someone like Joe Brennan was nothing to her now. Nothing except a professional contact.

Jennifer and Caroline went to Regine's together but, once there, went their separate ways. The entire first floor of the nightclub was packed with people talking in groups and weaving their way through the crowd. Once inside, Caroline happily turned to Jennifer and cried, "I'll see you later!"

The whole first floor, as Jennifer had read so many times, was decorated in shades of aubergine and silver, in an art deco pattern that was distinctive yet subtle. The decorations didn't overwhelm one's view or impressions of the guests. The pinkish tablecloths and soft lighting cast an attractive glow, making everyone look just that much prettier, handsomer, and even healthier.

Jennifer saw several familiar faces, and was making her way toward a group from Civette when she saw Joe leaning nonchalantly against a wall not fifteen feet from where she stood.

For a fleeting moment she considered pretending she hadn't seen him. But as soon as the impulse had occurred to her, she knew it was too late. For he was

47

smiling, no, grinning, she realized, and looking at her as if there were no one else in the room.

She managed to return the smile and began making her way through the crowd toward where he stood. Each time she looked up, his eyes met hers. And each time his eyes met hers, her heart quickened.

When she reached him he picked up two glasses from the edge of the table nearby and handed one to her. "I've been waiting for you," he said. "Scotch and soda all right?"

"Yes, it's my drink," she answered.

"I know," he answered, smiling. "I got a whiff of it when we had our fateful meeting by the elevator at the St. Moritz. And I remembered."

She tilted her head. "But you didn't know who I was then."

He took a slow deep breath, his eyes roving across her face, over her breasts, to her mouth, to her eyes. "Does it matter?" he asked softly. "When I notice a woman," he murmured, his gaze holding hers, "I notice at some level, subliminally perhaps, everything about her—her eyes, her lips, the way she moves, her scent"—he smiled—"including her drink, if she has one."

"Ah," she answered dreamily. For a moment she was taken back to that time six years ago when she had ached for him to look at her like this, dreamed of it night after night, but then she caught herself and looked away. "Well! They've got quite a crowd this year. Caroline told me you bought tickets for everyone at the company."

"I like to do what I can for everyone at Eton when I can."

"Mmm. I can imagine," she said doubtfully.

He pursed his lips and looked at her thoughtfully. "Difficult as it is for you to believe, Miss Preston, I do treat my employees as well as I possibly can. And I have more than personal vanity at stake when I ask you to believe me, Jennifer, because I'd very much like you to join us at Eton. Very much."

"I've already told you, Joe. I'm very happy at Civette."

His gaze penetrated hers. "Not as happy as you'd be at Eton," he said softly.

"I see you haven't lost any of your confidence over the past six years, Joe. I don't know what makes you so certain you're right."

"*You* do," he murmured, his voice gentle and caressing.

She took a sip of her drink. "I don't know what you're talking about," she said quietly, wishing his eyes weren't so blue.

"It's in your eyes, and your manner, and my memory of a younger you at Essences—"

"That younger me is gone, Joe," she cut in. "I've done more than six years of growing up since then. I was very young and very naive."

He tilted his head. "What about that exit speech you delivered?" he asked. "About how you had worked so hard, about how you had learned all you could—"

"It was true then," she said, "but then I was counting on you. I had wrongly thought you could be some sort of mentor, a model I could follow and

49

work with. The hard work was fine, but that was all that was. I was very innocent."

He looked at her questioningly. "But I was right then, wasn't I? You would have never been able to advance as far as you have if you had stayed at Essences."

She drew herself up to her full height. "I can hardly believe you still persist in patting yourself on the back, Joe. I know now that what happened wasn't the tragedy I had thought it was at the time. But the fact that I've come far hardly gives you license to justify your actions."

"Still angry then, aren't you?"

She sighed and shook her head. "No. I just remember, that's all. But how I seemed to you six years ago is hardly a reason for wanting to hire me now. It's just plain silly."

He smiled. "You must admit there are similarities —a certain confidence and determination, for instance." He paused. "In those deep gray eyes. Your lower lip."

"What about my lower lip?" she demanded.

He smiled. "You're doing it now. A near-pout, something that can be done only by someone with a mouth as lovely as yours."

She glared. "Stop it," she said half-seriously.

He shook his head. "No." He smiled. "Your voice, too, I remember it now . . . half-angry, half with the promise that you don't really mean it."

"Oh, come on."

He grinned. "Although sometimes you do, obviously." His eyes swept over her face, her hair. "What was your hair like then? I can't quite—oh, yes—

50

curly—sweet, but not quite you." He took in the rest of her slowly, from her head to her toes. "And you certainly have filled out since then in rather nice ways."

Her eyes widened. "I asked you to stop," she said, coloring under his amused scrutiny. "But since you don't seem to be able to, Joe"—she raised her glass in a toast—"cheers, and I'll see you later."

She turned to leave, but he caught her by the arm. "Wait."

His grip was strong. She turned around and met his eyes. "What the hell do you think you're doing?" she demanded.

He let her go immediately and his lips parted in surprise. "I'm sorry," he said, shaking his head. "I didn't mean to grab you like that."

"Then why did you?" she flared, but instantly regretted her words when her eyes met his. Their deep blue drew her into their depths, captured her as if forever.

"Where are you going?" he asked softly.

She shrugged. "I don't know. To get some of that food, to start. I had meetings all day and haven't eaten since breakfast."

"Well, you can't eat here," he stated.

"And why not?"

"Because it's far too crowded. You'll have to eat standing up with all these people around, and it will be quicker, I guarantee, at even the slowest restaurant in town. Now, I have to put in an appearance here for a while—as do you—so let's share a dance, nod our hellos, and go."

"I don't think—"

"Artichokes vinaigrette, celery rémoulade, beef Perigordine, the best French bread I've ever had in my life, Margaux forty-seven, and a fresh raspberry tart with crème fraiche," he said.

Her mouth was watering. Suddenly the reasons for all the resistance—suspicion, wariness, mistrust—seemed much, much less important than the food Joe had just described. Without giving it much thought, she walked with him up toward the second floor, where, as Joe put it, the band was playing "civilized music" rather than the rock that was playing on the first floor.

As they started up the stairs he took her hand. Though it was a natural thing to do—it was nearly impossible to make one's way through the crowd—and though with someone else Jennifer might hardly have noticed the touch, now every cell in her body was aware of Joe's firm, strong grip, of the warmth of his skin, of a certain intimacy that called forth the kiss she so wanted to forget.

And when, seconds later, she slid into his arms and he guided her onto the dance floor, their bodies fit together as snugly and easily as their hands had clasped. Jennifer was aware of every inch of his body as he pressed her close, one warm, strong hand at the small of her back, his taut, lean thighs moving in perfect, easy rhythm with hers. And the scent that reached her and mesmerized her—she closed her eyes and inhaled it deeply—was powerfully Joe's own. It thrust her back to her time at Essences, when Joe had just developed it. It was just slightly woodsy and pure male, and it filled Jennifer with a flowing desire she had forgotten, as if this were then and she were still deeply attracted, deeply wanting his arms around her as they were now.

She was aware that his cheek was nestled into her hair, that she was holding him more tightly than she meant, but her cares floated away with the strains of the clarinet and gentle rhythm of the drums.

"You smell lovely," he murmured. "Chanel?"

"No, an experiment," she said dreamily. "Something we put together at the lab last week."

He held her tighter and eased her into the slightly quickened rhythm of the band. "I might be trying to pump some trade secrets out of you, you know."

"You won't succeed," she answered easily, settling her cheek into his strong shoulder.

She closed her eyes, falling into the delicious awareness that was only of the senses—of Joe's nearness and warmth, the sweet sounds of the band, the scent that mingled with her own.

Joe shifted slightly and drew his head back, and she found herself looking into his eyes as if in a trance.

"Are you ready?" he murmured, his gaze fusing with hers.

"For what?" she asked dreamily.

A glimmer of a smile appeared. "For dinner. Naturally."

She laughed. "Naturally. Yes, I'm famished."

He smiled broadly. "Sounds delicious," he said, and as the next melody began, he led her off the dance floor.

Joe and Jennifer were both so hungry when they arrived at the restaurant that they barely talked after they were seated, concentrating on the delicious French bread and fresh sweet butter rather than on each other. The lack of conversation was easy and natural and totally different from the awkward silences Jennifer had endured on dates over the years. Of course, this wasn't a date, she reminded herself.

After the waiter had taken their orders and Joe had approved the wine, he filled Jennifer's glass and smiled. "I've been thinking, by the way, about what you said to me at the office the other day—about the Ardence campaign. You don't mind talking business, by the way, do you?"

Jennifer shook her head. "No, not at all." She loved talking about her work virtually anywhere, anytime. Sometimes, she knew, she used her career and its problems as excuses to concentrate on business matters to the exclusion of important personal concerns. Many times in the past she had been so cold and so utterly businesslike with men from her own and other offices that she had completely snuffed out whatever personal interest they had had in her. She was aware of it, and didn't care one bit if others were as well. It was her life, and she could do what she wanted with it. So for once it was nice to have a man interested in seriously discussing business, one who didn't feel the need to make an excuse that he wasn't discussing a more "appropriate" topic.

"Well," Joe said, sipping his wine and looking at Jennifer with mischief in his eyes, "I don't honestly see why you were so sure of your point. You said the campaign was outdated. Now everyone wants to know who it is I spoke with who's so right when they're all so wrong."

Jennifer smiled. "Why didn't you just give them my name?"

"Would you have appreciated that? In any case, the point is not who you are, but whether or not what you're saying is true."

Jennifer took another sip of wine. She felt wonderful—warmed by the wine, lulled by the glow of the candlelight, mesmerized by the dancing light of Joe's eyes. "Everything I say is true," she murmured, and knew she was feeling the wine. Her smile was a bit crooked, she suspected, but what did it really matter?

"Would you mind explaining, then, to an old friend—or an old enemy?"

Jennifer smiled lazily, gazing into azure. "It's very simple," she began. "Women don't want fantasies that are so . . . obvious. They want to believe—as well they should— *this can happen to me*. They want to know that there's something, whether it's a fragrance, or an attitude, or a person, that can change their lives. They want to know they can meet a man they like—a real man. Not a pirate, appearing out of nowhere and sweeping them off their feet. They want to lead their lives in the hope that something good can happen, instead of wildly hoping for the impossible—in this case, a pirate."

Joe smiled. "Too good to be true?"

Jennifer laughed. "Maybe. I think it's a little silly. It just doesn't touch me."

He reached his hand forward then, and covered hers. When he spoke, his voice was a whisper-soft caress with a core of coaxing urgency. "What does, Jennifer? What touches you?"

When her eyes met his, she nearly melted into him, her lips parting in yearning.

His voice tugged at her, urged her, started the warmth and liquid flowing through her, quickened the beating of her heart. He gently stroked her hand, and the desire in his eyes mesmerized her.

"I—"

And then Joe looked up, and Jennifer saw that the waiter had appeared. Jennifer hadn't even noticed the man; but when Joe had turned away, the heaviness of longing, the mood that had enveloped them, had dissipated like smoke in a breeze.

Joe ordered raspberry *tartes maison* and then turned to Jennifer with the hint of a smile on his lips. "You were saying?" He raised an inquiring brow.

She took a sip of wine to cover the pause while she collected her thoughts; she wasn't, after all, about to sink back into that haze. "Well," she said lightly, "I really don't know how much more you need to know, Joe. You've simply done it all wrong; that's all there is to it. What you want to do is create a life-style scent, one that gives you a way to live, a style, a spirit—something that a woman can adopt as her own rather than relying on a designer to dictate her taste. All you've given is a picture of a pirate—it's too naive for today's women."

He shrugged. "Well, what would you suggest? Ardence—and we're changing the pronunciation to a French one—ar-DAHNS—when we start our television campaign. Anyway, Ardence suggests

56

spirit, heat, passion, and, to some extent, fantasy. I thought pirates fit."

Jennifer sighed and shook her head. "You have to show what that means in *today's* society, Joe. A woman on a horse galloping across the plains out West, racing a dune buggy along the surf in the East, skydiving over the mountains—anything. Some of the shots can be with a man, but the point is that the woman is in control of her life. And she's going to choose to be wild . . . free . . . open to adventure and to her own tastes and needs and desires in whatever way she wants."

He pursed his lips, barely suppressing a smile. "You sound as if the idea appeals to you."

She met his gaze fully. "It does . . . at times."

They looked into each other's eyes wordlessly.

"I'll make sure you get home safely then." The look in his eyes belied his words, for he knew—as did she—that neither would be safe with the other.

The rest of the meal—dessert and coffee—was spent much as at the beginning, quietly, with few words. But the mood had deepened, become laden with unspoken messages, tacit questions answered by meaningful glances and pauses, accidental touches, and unbroken gazes.

Yet, on leaving the restaurant, Joe neither took Jennifer's arm nor made any sort of advance. The same was true in the taxi going uptown, and Jennifer, with the wine's lulling effects rapidly dissipating, began to wonder if she had imagined the vibrations of mutual desire that had seemed so pervasive. But she knew she hadn't on her part, and she knew, too, that if Joe shared her feelings and impulses, she

57

would have to reject him. Joe turned himself on and off whenever he needed to. Even tonight he had been able to break a glance, a mood, whenever it struck him to do so. With all that she knew of him—from the past, from the day in his office at Eton—she was more than sufficiently aware that Joe used his charms capriciously.

Jennifer was momentarily distracted from her thoughts when she and Joe arrived at her apartment and Joe said how much he liked it. She was pleased; she had moved in only two months before, and Joe was the first guest she had had, aside from Caroline. Most of the furniture was modern, with simple lines and colors that were all variations on white and tan, except for a few bright splashes of color in the couch cushions.

"This must be a nice place to come home to after work," Joe said, standing against the railing that overlooked the sunken living room. He turned to Jennifer, who was standing, cautiously, she realized, a few paces back. "Your cousin Caroline lives here too?" he asked.

Jennifer nodded.

"Is she here?"

Jennifer smiled and shook her head. "Definitely not. I don't even have to look. With Caroline, you'd know if she were home even if this were a thirty-room apartment."

Joe laughed, but then grew serious. In the silence they exchanged looks of fire. "Then come here," he said quietly.

She stood rooted to the spot, torn. And then he came forward, his blue gaze locked with hers, and though part of Jennifer's mind tried to command her to protest, even to move away, she waited, melting with desire. He took her in his arms, his hands strong around the small of her back, and with a moan of deep need, covered her mouth with his own. The kiss was long, deep, urgent, as his tongue explored the inner warmth of her mouth with exquisite delicacy yet growing demand. As he tightened his grasp around her waist and pulled her close against his lean frame, he wrenched his mouth from hers and gazed deeply into her eyes. "I've been wanting to do this all night," he rasped, his lips grazing hers. "With you in my arms as we were dancing, my God, Jennifer. The way you held yourself so close, your breasts against my chest—" He edged his cheek along hers, his rough skin sending thrills of excitement through her. "You're more beautiful every time I see you, Jennifer, every time I touch you."

"Oh, Joe," she murmured moments before his lips joined with hers in a surge of desire that made her tremble and wrap her arms more tightly around him. The heat of his body made her ache with need.

"I want you," he grated, feeding her desire with his very voice, so filled with need it was like a searing touch. "I want you tonight. . . . I want you now."

"I can't," she murmured into his neck, her senses whirling as he moved his hands around the front of her, cupping her breasts, his fingers flicking and coaxing her nipples through the thin fabric of her dress. His lips descended on her neck, kissing and nipping until she was inflamed with a desperate craving. She wanted to feel his taut thighs part hers. She wanted to feel his coaxing, questing fingers bring her to heights of ecstasy. She wanted to merge with him in moaning, breathless need.

"Well, well!" came a voice. Caroline's, Jennifer dimly realized.

The door behind them slammed shut, and Jennifer and Joe broke their embrace like guilty teenagers.

Caroline was smiling crookedly, obviously having had more than a few drinks at Regine's, and stared unabashedly at Joe and Jennifer as she walked past them to the foyer closet. "So!" she said loudly.

Jennifer and Joe exchanged glances.

"I had the greatest time of my entire *life* tonight!" she cried, throwing her shawl into the closet. "Hi, Mr. Brennan, by the way."

"I think I'd better be going," Joe said in a voice that would brook no questions. "Good night, Jennifer. And good night, Caroline. See you at work in the morning."

He left quickly, not even casting one last look at Jennifer. When the door closed, it was so sudden. It had all been so quick, it was almost as if he hadn't been there, as if he had been a dream. For there had been no last look of longing, no good-bye kiss to mark his departure. Nothing, that is, except his lingering scent and the still deeply arousing physical memory of his touch—and the touch she had so wanted.

"Sorry if I broke anything up," Caroline said, half-dancing, half-walking down the steps and into the living room. "I just had the most divine evening though." She flopped onto the couch and watched as Jennifer came to join her. "Do you know a guy named Tim Somers?" she asked.

"Yes, I do," Jennifer answered. She was annoyed at Caroline's total lack of sensitivity to her interruption, but was too tired and disoriented to say anything. And in a way she welcomed the distraction, for any topic other than Joe seemed simple. "I, uh, don't know him well though. Isn't he marketing director at Ilana Cosmetics? Blond, sort of Scandinavian-looking?"

Caroline smiled. "Yeah. Great-looking, you might say. I danced with him all night, Jennifer. *And* we're going to go out—maybe to dinner or something. Isn't that great?" She frowned. "What's the matter? Why are you looking at me as if I just told you I was going out with Attila the Hun?"

Jennifer laughed. "I'm sorry, Caroline. I didn't mean to. I just don't know Tim Somers too well, and—"

"And you're not my chaperon," Caroline interrupted. "So please don't worry about me. I can take care of myself."

Jennifer sighed and nodded. "You're right," she said. "And I'm glad you had fun."

Caroline smiled and sat up straighter. "So tell me about your evening with the big boss. I thought you weren't going to have anything to do with him, Jennifer."

"I'm not going to," Jennifer answered, as much to herself as to her cousin. "I just happened to spend some time with him tonight, that's all. We both wanted to go out and eat, so—"

"So you came back here to make out." Caroline winked. "I get the picture, Jennifer. And I think it's

61

great. Now I have a real in at the company in case anything goes wrong—"

"Now, wait a minute," Jennifer cut in. "You most certainly do not. What you saw tonight was meaningless."

"It didn't look so meaningless to me," Caroline answered.

"Oh, you know what I mean. The point is that I don't trust him, he probably doesn't trust me, and the time we spent together was purely . . ." Her voice trailed off. She could hardly say "purely professional." "Well, it was just meaningless, that's all," she finished impatiently. "So forget it." *And any plans you might have to take advantage of it,* she added silently to herself.

"Okay, okay," Caroline answered. "God. I didn't ask for the Gettysburg Address, Jennifer." She tilted her head. "I'd just like to know one thing though."

"What's that?"

"Don't you ever let your guard down?"

Jennifer sighed. "It's late," she said, looking at her watch. "We could both use some sleep." And she went into her bedroom, put the pile of Caroline's sheets and blanket on a chest in the hallway, and went to get ready for bed.

Caroline's question disturbed her in more ways than one. Naturally Jennifer had asked the question of herself many times. She had had few relationships with men over the years, few close friendships with women. Caroline was someone she hadn't seen in fifteen or so years, and even she had noticed the protective armor Jennifer had constructed around herself.

62

Jennifer sighed as she looked into the mirror, her pale eyes filled with doubt. But as she recalled the evening, from its beginning to end, she remembered how she had felt earlier about the contrast between herself and her cousin. She was older, wiser, and, on the whole, probably happier than Caroline. Perhaps Caroline met more people, went out more frequently. But was there anything so "right" or wonderful about her life? She had been swept off her feet by Tim Somers, a man Jennifer hardly knew but didn't like the looks of. Caroline was happy, but how long would it last?

Jennifer closed her eyes. She knew she sounded bitter, critical, and self-righteous. Just what was she fighting?

FOUR

Two weeks after the charity ball Jennifer was quickly flipping through *Women's Wear Daily* at the office—she rarely had time to read it carefully until she got home—when she noticed an item that nearly jumped out at her from the page:

> Eton alters new campaign; drops agency in Brennan Brainstorm.

Jennifer brushed her bangs back from her face and read on:

> Joseph Brennan, new president of Eton Cosmetics (see page 26) has dropped Thorpe/McKay/Kendall as its agency, leaving it in the dust as a mere media-buying service. "We're going in-house from now on," says Brennan, "starting with our campaign for Ardence, our newest

women's fragrance line. We simply feel that we have a better understanding of our product than any agency," Brennan said, adding that he was "basically pleased" with T/McK/K's work but felt it was "time for a change." The move marks the third of such changes in New York's cosmetics industry, in which the roles of in-house marketing personnel are gaining ever-increasing importance. The new Ardence campaign (see page 34) is Brennan's own brainchild, inspired, Brennan says, "by a deep belief in the loveliness of Ardence and a deep desire to have it reach its proper market. We hope to create a campaign whose success will rival that of other successful 'life-style' fragrances, and have every confidence that we'll be able to do so." Art Caulfield, v.p. creative of T/McK/K, commented in a brief telephone interview that there had been "no dissatisfaction on Brennan's part that we knew of until we got a call Monday morning," but that T/McK/K would continue as Eton's media buyer for all print and broadcast media. Cosmetics news continues on page 23.

Jennifer turned to the page on which Joe's campaign was making its debut, and there it was, literally word-for-word and image-for-image what Jennifer had described to Joe a week earlier. It was amazing that he had been able to get the campaign together that quickly—almost unbelievable—but Jennifer knew that with Joe, anything was possible when it came to work. Anything including shameless stealing.

The ad was beautiful. A pretty young woman with long black hair and gray eyes was in all three pictures, galloping across the sand on a gray-and-white horse, parachuting over rolling green hills, racing along the beach in a buggy, with the surf wild and untamed in the background. "Live in the heat of the moment, in the spirit that's yours and yours alone," the words read across the pictures. There was a square of black folded over the edge of the page, and Jennifer lifted it. There, underneath, was a picture of the same gray-eyed young woman, but this time she was in a gray suit, in an office that looked remarkably like Eton's. She was in the arms of—or rather had in *her* arms—a tall, dark-haired man, and she was brushing her lips along his neck in a sensual kiss. Underneath it read, "You can be wild in spirit anywhere, anytime. The choice is up to you. Ardence— the scent, the life-style."

Jennifer smiled. It was an undeniably good ad, exactly what the scent required. Joe's addition had helped it considerably, linking the concept to both romance and day-to-day living. Yet the idea had been hers, even the idea to scrap the old ad had been hers, when she had just been idly speculating, and he had carried it all out to the letter.

She leaned back in her chair and tried to remember. Just why *had* she given him all that advice? He was a major competitor, after all—not a friend, not a colleague at her company.

She remembered that she had initially criticized the Ardence ad back at his office, but little had been said then. It was only at Regine's—or *after* Regine's, at the French restaurant—that she had really begun to let loose. He had wined her and dined her, as the saying goes, and she had fallen into his trap as easily as he could possibly have hoped for.

She picked up the phone and buzzed her secretary. "Sherry, could you please get me Joe Brennan at Eton—and hold all calls."

"Yes, Jennifer."

She bit her lip as she waited, unwelcome memories flooding her mind. How embarrassing . . . that kiss, all those glances. She had fallen for it all as if she were still the twenty-two-year-old starry-eyed young woman of years before. Though she had thought she had been strong, though she had thought she had resisted, she had fallen wholeheartedly and blindly for his line.

"Mr. Brennan is on line two, Jennifer."

"Thanks, Sherry." She pressed the lit button on the phone and said, "Congratulations on the campaign, Joe. And the article. You must be very pleased with yourself."

"I am," he said. She could practically hear him smiling. "And the board of directors is quite pleased, too. This sort of thing is exactly what they had in mind when they brought me in." He paused. "You should be pleased, too, at its reception."

"Why on earth should I be pleased to see a competitor race—my God, Joe, you must have set a record with this one—*race* an ad into print using all my ideas?"

"Why on earth, one could ask, did you give them to me?"

"Oh, come on, Joe. I didn't think you were going to rush out and set up a shooting the next day, for goodness' sake! We were just talking over dinner. Your campaign was done. Finished."

"Ah, I see. Then business can be conducted only within the four walls of an office, and romance within the four walls of a bedroom, and—"

"Damn it, Joe, you're completely obscuring the point. I—"

"The point, my dear Jennifer, is that we all know —you as well as I—that this is how business works. No one person can be credited with an idea or its execution. And sometimes—though not often—an idea may come from a competitor. I'm a businessman, Jennifer, and I merely acted on your excellent advice. You could have been part of Eton when you gave the advice. That you weren't was your decision, but at the time, it didn't concern me."

Jennifer knew that he was right, in the larger sense. In his position she might very well have done what he had. But she would never have led anyone on emotionally or sexually. And her emotional state was what had blinded her that night to what she was doing. Yet there was no point in dwelling on it. It hadn't been the best move of her career. "Look, Joe," she said. "We might as well forget the whole thing, all right?"

"My offer still stands, you know."

"And my answer still stands. Good-bye, Joe."

"Jennifer—"

"Good-bye," she said firmly, and hung up.

That evening, when Caroline came home from the office, the whole incident was brought forth again as Caroline babbled on about the new Ardence campaign. Jennifer said nothing about her contribution

—her foolish mistake was best forgotten. The fact that the idea had been hers seemed less and less important as Caroline went on about its effects on the company. Morale was good for the first time in months, according to Caroline's coworkers, and everyone was feeling like part of a team.

As Caroline talked, Jennifer remembered how part of what she had admired in Joe so many years ago had been his almost ruthless ambition, his willingness to take risks in order to achieve a goal. She had, in fact, modeled her own behavior on his to some extent over the years. And she saw more clearly than ever that what bothered her about what had happened was not what Joe had done, but how unaware she had been. And how foolishly, easily, and unseeingly she had fallen into his arms and succumbed to a kiss—and a temptation—that meant nothing to the man.

Jennifer was so lost in thought that she hadn't noticed Caroline had switched topics and was now chattering away about Tim Somers and where they were going that night.

"Did you hear me?" Caroline asked.

"What? Oh, I'm sorry, Caroline, no."

Caroline rolled her eyes. "I *said* that Tim is taking me to Elaine's, Jennifer. Isn't that great? That's where *everyone* goes—famous people, rich people, the whole bit."

Jennifer laughed.

Caroline stood up. "Well, I'd better get ready. Tim's picking me up downstairs in half an hour." She sighed. "But you know? Every time I go out with him, I feel weird going out—you're always working or going to some professional-type function or your dance class or something, and I sometimes wonder. Maybe I should work harder and play a little less."

Jennifer smiled. "Don't be silly. You should do what you want. And have fun."

Caroline smiled uncertainly. "Yeah, I guess you're right."

A week later, Caroline announced that she was moving out, into a little apartment on York Avenue she had found, five blocks from Jennifer's.

Jennifer raised a brow. "That must be pretty expensive, Caroline. Are you sure you can afford it?"

Caroline turned scarlet. "Well, I figure if I scrimp on clothes and eat yogurt instead of sandwiches and stuff during the day, I might be able to swing it. And if I can't, maybe I'll take in a roommate or something. It's a one-bedroom."

"Hmm. I'm impressed. Well, congratulations." She smiled. "I know you'll love it." She knew, too, that she would love having Caroline off her hands. Though Caroline wasn't really any trouble, it was annoying having someone sleeping out in the living room all the time. And Jennifer didn't enjoy playing housemother four out of every five mornings, when Caroline slept through her alarm and Jennifer had to wake her up. The one aspect of Caroline's moving out that made Jennifer uncomfortable was the high rent Caroline had mentioned. Yogurt or no yogurt, there was no way Caroline could possibly afford a studio—much less a one-bedroom—on the paltry salary Joe paid.

And then she suspected, indeed, almost knew, how Caroline could afford the apartment—Tim Somers.

"Caroline, is everything okay? I mean, is there anything you want to tell me, or talk about?"

Caroline shrugged uncertainly. "No, I—everything's really good. I mean I should be really happy, right? I've got a job in New York, a new apartment, a boyfriend who's right out of a magazine. What more could I want?" She shrugged again. "I mean, my job isn't the greatest." She sighed. "In fact, I might quit. But aside from that—"

"Wait a minute. Slow down," Jennifer interrupted. "What do you mean, you might quit? Do you have another offer?"

Caroline looked down at her hands. "Well, no. I asked Tim if I could work at his place, but he said he wanted me to stay at Eton for a while. It looks bad to be hopping around all the time, you know." She sighed. "It's just . . . I hate the atmosphere. Everything's back to its old boring routine, and that Joe Brennan is a real pain."

Jennifer frowned. "What do you mean?"

"Oh, he just . . . I don't know. He doesn't treat us very well, and—"

"I thought you had said he was great. He bought those tickets for the charity ball—"

"That's just the point. It's paternalistic. Instead of buying us tickets to some ball, he should raise our salaries. Tim says Joe's famous for treating people like dirt."

"What does he know?" Jennifer demanded. "Has he ever worked for Joe?"

"Well, no. But you said—"

"What I said, Caroline, has nothing to do with *you*. I had a bad experience with Joe many years ago, but that's for me to take care of. That shouldn't influence you in any way."

Caroline shrugged. "Well—"

The phone rang, and Caroline jumped. "Maybe that's Tim," she said breathlessly, and ran across the living room to answer it. "Oh. Yes," she said coldly. "I'll see." She clapped her hand over the receiver and turned to Jennifer. "Speak of the pain himself. Are you in for Joe Brennan?"

Jennifer's heart jumped. "Yes," she said. "Yes, of course."

A few moments later she hung up, having made a date for that evening. "A business meeting," Joe had assured her, "so you can be properly on your guard against me."

Jennifer had laughed, but with a pang she realized it was the second time in only a few weeks that she had been described as on her guard. She knew she was too cautious, too wary of people, but she didn't think she could change. As a child she hadn't made friends easily. Her mother had worried at first, but her father had pointed out that she was "just waitin' till she was sure, and then she gets the best." Later on, with boys in high school and men in college and afterward, Jennifer accepted far fewer invitations than she received. She simply didn't have particularly good feelings about any but a few of the men she met. And so far, even with those, the relationships had always ended in disappointment of one sort or another.

As Jennifer was good at pushing things she didn't

want to consider to the back of her mind, most of the time she didn't let the fact that she was alone bother her. What kept gnawing against the edges of her consciousness, though, and stubbornly refused to leave, was the notion—the fact—that she had never had a truly satisfying relationship with a man. For her, the definition did not have to include marriage— she simply didn't see marriage as any great necessity. What the definition *did* include, and what she had never experienced, was a really satisfying sexual relationship. Even with the last man she had dated, Andrew Cole, a colleague from Civette, she had thought she loved him, and she had made love with him many times. But somehow, rather than making the relationship better, the lovemaking made it worse—for Jennifer realized she didn't love Andrew, and, soon afterward, broke the relationship off.

Yet she remembered what she had *almost* felt, and knew she was being unfair to herself by making her life so narrow. True, her life didn't have to be packed with men and adventure, but it didn't have to be all work either. Perhaps tonight she could experiment with a new Jennifer. She'd try to be less serious, more relaxed, less wary. When it came to the business Joe wanted to discuss—he had mentioned something about making her a "better offer" for working at Eton—she would be as wary as she had ever been. But perhaps she could try to relax a bit more when they weren't discussing business; perhaps she could get to know Joe Brennan, the man . . . and Jennifer Preston, the woman, as well.

But Jennifer was on her guard almost immediately. From the moment Joe had arrived to pick her up at her apartment, he had had a gleam in his eye, a spark that warned her he was up to something. He had said only that he'd "present his case" when the time was right, and gazed at Jennifer with such unabashed pleasure that she turned away.

Once seated at the restaurant, a tiny French country-style place near Jennifer's apartment, Joe captured Jennifer's gaze and spoke. "I've thought of calling you," he began. "I've thought of it almost every day since I last spoke with you."

Something in Jennifer shifted, began to melt, but she ignored it.

"I didn't call you at the office because I thought you might still be annoyed. And most of all, because I don't think that's our best arena." He looked into her eyes. "Sometimes I'd rather hear Jennifer than Ms. Preston. I'd rather hear you laugh than speak in that very professional manner you have." He paused. "I'd rather see you showing that part of yourself you so rarely reveal."

Jennifer raised a brow. "I can assure you, Joe, that the 'professional' side of me is very real."

He looked at her speculatively. "You're doing it right now," he said softly. "We're not at the office, Jennifer."

He was making her nervous. He was too smooth, too swift, like a wild, flowing river after a heavy rain, a river that could sweep her away. "I thought you said this was a business dinner," she said coolly.

He sighed and shook his head. "All right. I'll get right to it then. As soon as we order. Do you know what you want?"

74

"Uh, yes," she said absently. He had switched gears in seconds, from being smooth and relaxed, persuasive and coaxing, to abrupt and cold. She could hardly blame him though. What was wrong with her?

"I recommend the moules marinières," he said. "They're excellent."

"Oh. Then you've been here before?"

He nodded. "About a dozen times or so. My girl friend and I used to come here all the time."

"Ah." It was odd to hear him say "my girl friend." Unsettling.

When she looked up he was looking at her. "We broke up three months ago," he said.

"Ah."

His lips curled into a smile. "You're uncharacteristically quiet all of a sudden, Jennifer." He raised a brow. "Have I said something wrong?"

She felt her cheeks beginning to color. "No, no. Of course not." God! Why was she blushing like a teenager?

"Tell me," he said quietly, "if you don't mind my asking. You've never been married, have you?"

She shook her head.

"I guess you know I haven't been either." He smiled sadly. "The next question is always 'Why not?' But don't you find there is no one answer? It isn't simply 'I haven't found the right person,' or 'I've devoted myself to my work,' or even an earlier love affair that didn't work out. These days, people just don't seem to get married that quickly . . . or easily."

"Well, with one in two or three marriages ending in divorce, it's easy to understand," she put in.

He shrugged. "I don't think people avoid it because of the statistics, Jennifer. People are afraid, that's all. I know every serious relationship I've had over the past several years has been constricting in some way. Women have made demands I just couldn't meet—that sort of thing."

"Unreasonable demands?" she asked.

He shook his head quickly. "No, not at all. Most of the women I've dated have had good reason to be dissatisfied to some degree. Only I've never been willing to provide the solution—to work less, be more domestic, whatever. And I've never wanted commitment the way most women do. I don't know whether that's because of the women I've been with, or just me, but it's always been true." He tilted his head. "And I sense it's true with you too. A certain wariness, a holding-back quality you have."

Jennifer's heart quickened. She suddenly felt put on the spot, under examination. "I think," she began, trying to collect her thoughts, "I think it's just a matter of finding the right person. Then everything else falls into place."

Their eyes met, and Joe smiled. "Well. We haven't exactly been talking about business, have we." He frowned. "How did we get on to *marriage?*"

Jennifer laughed. "I don't know," she said, her eyes shining. "But it's nice, actually. It's such a pleasure talking to someone who's not Caroline."

He laughed. "She's a sweet kid though."

"Mmm. You make me feel guilty for being glad she's moving out."

He reached forward and tilted her chin so she was looking at him. His eyes were deep and serious. "Don't ever feel guilty," he said softly, "for what you know is right." His eyes roved over her face—to her mouth, her cheeks, her hair, her eyes. He inhaled deeply. "Don't ever feel guilty," he murmured, "or deny what you know is true."

She had to look away from those eyes—she commanded herself to do so—and finally she did, and gazed down at the tablecloth.

His warm hand covered hers then, and she met his gaze.

"Joe—"

"I want you," he murmured. "I've been fighting with myself since I first saw you that day at the St. Moritz." He stroked her hand, her arm, sending a pulsating wave of warmth through her. "I wanted you for Eton, and I wanted you for . . . myself." His words made her warm with desire. "I wanted you to be a woman to me." For a moment the image of her body meshed with his flashed through her mind— sighing, clasping, moving together in perfect rhythm. "And someone who works with me as well." He gently turned her hand over and traced light patterns on her palm. It was a simple, exquisitely delicate touch, yet it sent tremors through her. He held her with his eyes, and she felt the gentle but insistent pressure of his knee against hers. She could imagine it parting her legs, coaxing her to a pitch of ecstasy. "I see things in your eyes, Jennifer, in the parting of your lips, the way your breath catches when I touch you, yet you hold back in every way." His gaze penetrated hers. "I don't make a habit of being where I'm

77

not wanted, or trying to make love with a woman who doesn't want me." He drew in a long breath. "But I've thought about you, Jennifer, during the day"—he paused—"and, in a very different way, at night. I don't know whether you've thought of me or not—" She imagined him in her arms, flesh against flesh, the rough texture of his chest raking her skin. "But I'd like to know. Am I wrong, or am I right to be hoping and waiting and wanting." His next words were almost a whisper. "Am I right, Jennifer?"

"Yes," she heard herself say, breathlessly, almost inaudibly.

He squeezed her hand. "I'm so glad," he answered. "I'm so glad," he repeated quietly.

Yet, almost as soon as she had spoken, Jennifer regretted her words. She had been mesmerized, drawn in by his touch, drowned in the azure depths of his eyes, lulled by the insistent but smooth pull of his voice. And suddenly she felt as if she had just awakened from a dream. She didn't, in fact, even know what she had agreed to. All she knew was that there was only one word she could say—yes—when his eyes penetrated hers, when the waves of desire his slightest touch created coursed through her with ardent need.

"Jennifer." Joe's voice cut through her thoughts.

"Yes, Joe."

"I'm glad you agreed to meet with me tonight." He paused. "If I come on strong, it's because it's the only way I know how to get what I want. I thought that tonight we could talk about your working at Eton—my plans, the plans you have for yourself—but right now, I think we've touched upon something more important." He drew in his breath. "I'd like it if we could just talk, get to know each other a little more."

And talk they did, long into the night, though there were pauses, silences edged with need, accidental caresses filled with desire. Each time their eyes met, a message more eloquent than any combination of words seemed to pass between them. Each time their hands would brush, knees would meet, breaths would catch at the same moment, each was thinking the same thing. *How good we'll be together.*

Occasionally, distracted by sounds of the restaurant or voices at the next table, Jennifer would wonder what had happened, how she had fallen into a heated web of yearning with this man, how they could communicate with the smallest glance. And when had she set aside her fears, her cautions, her wariness?

But by the end of the evening her questions were gone when Joe took her hand and they left the restaurant. They walked slowly, leisurely, lazily back to her apartment, the slow pace born of the knowledge they shared, the knowledge that said they would fall into each other's arms in minutes.

In the elevator they gazed into each other's eyes, only half aware that others were there too.

When Jennifer opened the door to her apartment, she was keenly aware of Joe's presence behind her, his body fitted close against hers.

When they stepped in to the foyer he closed the door, and with a hoarse moan pulled her against him. His mouth closed over hers, his tongue entering her warm, yielding mouth with an urgency borne of the hours of waiting and the waves of desire that had been building in each of them.

He tore his mouth from hers and scooped her up in his arms and carried her toward the living room. She roved her mouth over his neck, whispering his name, aching.

When he lay her on the couch he knelt beside her, and she looked up at him. His eyes were blazing with hunger.

"My God, how I want you," he said hoarsely. "Those eyes, Jennifer, you don't even know what you do with them." His own eyes closed, and with a groan he covered her lips with his, then trailed his mouth along her neck, his fingers tracing circles against her blouse. He raised his head and began opening the buttons, his eyes filled with the fire of arousal.

As his fingers worked she studied his face—a face etched with need, dark with passion, lit only by the moonlight coming through the window. He was all light and shadow, rough dark skin and soft smooth lips, silky hair and rough cheeks, tender touch and deep, urgent coaxing. He moved on top of her, his body firm and strong and warm, conveying a need she deeply wanted to satisfy, a need that fiercely matched her own.

He parted her unbuttoned blouse and moved downward, trailing his mouth over the rise of her breasts, across each nipple, fleetingly and temptingly. His skin was excitingly rough, his breath warm and damp, and his breathing fast, and her passion mounted as each inch of him touched her, at each lick of the tongue, each gentle bite, each hoarse breath hot against her skin.

His stroking fingers swelled her nipples to excitement, and she arched to find his every inch, to fit his coaxing male frame to her yielding, aching body. She wanted him as she never had—desperately, the waves of desire swamping her senses with need. He moved his hands downward then, in delicate caresses that grew increasingly urgent, increasingly exciting as he sought the smooth skin of her thighs. And then he parted them and she felt the hardness of his thighs, the urgency of his need as he moaned and whispered her name. "I want you so much," he rasped, his breath hot in her ear.

"I want you," she whispered. His hand kneaded her thigh, liquefying her with his fierce desire. She ran her hands along his back, holding him close, thinking, *This is the man I've wanted for so long, the man who's perfect for me, his desire as strong as my own.* And then she froze, her body tensing in fear. Joe *did* want something from her aside from the pleasures of lovemaking, and she had forgotten how he knew her weak points, her vulnerabilities, her aching, instant acquiescence to his caresses. And he was using her desire to his advantage. "Joe," she whispered.

"Yes, darling." He kissed her neck, her collarbone, the rise of her breasts. "Relax."

Jennifer closed her eyes, her senses whirling. "We have to stop," she said, her voice catching.

"What's the matter?" he asked quietly.

"It's . . . too soon," she murmured. She told herself her words were true, that no matter how good his

81

coaxing desire felt, how right it felt to be in his arms, it was too early to make love.

She shook her head. "I'm sorry, Joe. I didn't mean for it . . . for us . . . to go that far." She shook her head again. "It's just too soon for me. Too quick."

He sighed, his lips tightening. Then he lowered his head to her breasts, and she could feel the soft brush of his lashes against her skin as he closed his eyes.

"I'm sorry as hell that you feel that way," he said finally, his voice still hoarse with desire. He raised his head and looked into her eyes. "It's a hell of a way to end an evening, Jennifer. But I don't want you ever to do anything you don't want to do." He inhaled deeply. "No matter how carried away we get. And at least"—he smiled gently—"at least we've had a taste of things I hope will soon be ours."

She closed her eyes and smiled lazily. "I'm glad you feel that way, Joe," she said, stretching under his weight.

"And I'm very glad you're you—such a warm, beautiful, *sexy* woman." He playfully ran a finger down her forehead to the tip of her nose. "When the time is right, I'm going to enjoy making love to you very much."

She had to laugh then at the tone his voice had taken, half licentious, half achingly wistful. "Is that a threat, or a promise?" she teased.

"Just the right measure of both, my dear."

He shifted his weight and wrapped his arms around her, stroking her hair as she nestled close to him, her cheek against his chest. They lay together quietly that way for a long while, the deep rhythm of Joe's breathing, the warmth of his body molded to

82

the contours of her own, lulling her into a sense of utter contentment and tranquility. *Yes, this is good,* she thought hazily, *good and right.* She felt as if, held in Joe's arms this way, she had moved into a softly glowing world, a world she always imagined, but one which had somehow always eluded her.

"It's getting late, Jen," Joe whispered finally, his warm breath brushing a strand of hair by her ear.

"Hmm." She forced herself to sit up and then yawned sleepily.

He smiled down at her, his arms still draped lazily across her shoulder. "I know you're half asleep, but before I go there is something I still need to talk to you about. Your coming on at Eton. I think there are things you should know—things that could convince you, and we should talk seriously before you say no. Now, I'm going out of town for three weeks—we're opening a plant in Fort Worth—but when I get back, I'd like to really talk"—he smiled—"if we possibly can do that without getting distracted."

Jennifer sighed. "Listen, Joe. I don't see any point in keeping you wondering, when I already know what my answer is."

Uncertainty clouded his eyes. "Why?" he asked softly, his fingertips kneading her shoulder. "Why does it have to be no?"

She looked into his eyes. "If . . . if we're going to be involved, Joe, I think it's better to keep things simple, as uncomplicated as possible. I went out for a long time with a man I worked with once, and when we broke up, it was really rough. One of us had to leave."

Joe half-smiled. "And he was the one. And you're

afraid that if that happened with us, you'd be the one."

"Well, naturally. As president of Eton, you'd hardly go yourself, would you." She smiled, but her smile faded as he said his next words.

"Don't you think it's a bit early to worry about things like that?" He frowned as he paused. "I ... we're both rather cautious people, Jen. I wouldn't want to see you turn a wonderful opportunity down —wonderful for both of us—because you're afraid that things might not work out between us." He sighed. "I'm sorry, Jen. I can't seem to find the right words. But this *is* only the second time we've gone to dinner. Don't you think—"

"I think we'd better forget the whole subject," Jennifer said quietly. She had been planning to say more, but her throat was closing over her words.

She felt horribly disappointed, for Joe had been honest, but had spoken a truth she didn't want to hear. She didn't know what she had expected from him—or from herself—but casual sex was one thing she didn't want.

She shouldn't have forgotten whom she was dealing with. Joe Brennan was not a man of commitment —except in business—and she hadn't given him any indication that she either expected him or wanted him to be. And perhaps she didn't. All she knew was that if she were going to be more involved with him, she would have to know him—and trust him— much, much more than she did at the moment.

"What's the matter?" Joe asked softly, stroking her cheek. "We can talk more when I come back."

She nodded. "Right. But forget about the job, all

right? It's just silly to keep batting the idea around."
Her words had come out more harshly than she had
meant them to, but she didn't soften them with a
touch or even a glance. She was angry—both at herself and at Joe—and she needed time to think.

FIVE

Joe had been tender and caring when he had left that evening, leaving Jennifer to wonder whether she hadn't overreacted to his words about things "not working out." Most likely it was her pride that had been wounded, for she was as wary of emotional involvement and commitment as he was.

Yet, as the days went by and the nights were warm and ripe with memories and longings, Jennifer couldn't help remembering . . . and even missing Joe. She was surprised, for she didn't, in fact, know him all that well. But they had talked of many things that night—childhood, hopes, fears—and she couldn't forget the new side of Joe she had glimpsed.

But she eventually thought less about him as pressures at her job increased. Difficult as her problems at work were, they seemed easier to tackle than problems of the heart.

Jennifer had just won a battle with one of the

vice-presidents of Civette, and the advertising budget she had requested for their new shampoo/hair-care line had been approved. It was strange, actually, how easily she had won. Usually her disagreements with top management were resolved only after days of long meetings and telephone conversations. Just as Jennifer had been gearing up for a huge fight, the v.p., Arlen Davis, had sent a terse memo back saying she had the okay. Odd.

Later that day Jennifer heard Davis was leaving. Wherever she looked on the eighth floor, where most of the corporate offices were, faces were ashen, stricken, and pale.

At the end of the day she heard the news. Civette was being acquired by Jenneco, Inc., a large pharmaceuticals firm, and no one knew who was staying on and who was leaving. But the general consensus was that Davis had been the first of what were going to be many, many casualties.

By the next morning, the news was all over—in *The New York Times, The Wall Street Journal, Women's Wear Daily,* and all the trades. Jennifer had spent the previous evening making lists of her assets, her debts, and the most important list of all, her contacts. She wrote several versions of the last list—companies, people, products. And Joe Brennan and Eton were always at the top of each list.

Though Jennifer didn't like the idea, she knew what she had to do. Jobs at her level in her industry simply weren't that easy to come by. Corporate search firms had called her several times over the past few years, asking if she wanted to leave Civette and dangling very attractive offers in front of her.

But she hadn't had a call in months—the job market was dry—and she simply couldn't afford what would perhaps be months between jobs. *If* her job at Civette were eliminated—but from all viewpoints, it looked very, very likely. No, she couldn't just sit around waiting for the ax to fall.

She would go back to working with Joe Brennan.

Her immediate image was of him sitting behind his desk, arms crossed, grinning in smug satisfaction. But the image didn't fit, didn't make sense. She had learned enough about Joe to know he wouldn't hold out her decision as one she had been slow to come to, when he had known all along. No, either Joe had changed or she had changed, and she suspected each had grown in ways they hadn't realized over the past years.

When she called Joe two days later upon his return to the city, he sounded surprised to hear from her, and then said, "Ah-ha, then." She could hear that he was smiling. "It all becomes clear, ladies and gentlemen. I heard about the shakeup down at Civette, Jennifer. Is that what's up?"

"Well, yes," she said. "As a matter, of fact, Joe—"

"The job is yours," he interrupted. "And I'm very glad, Jennifer. When I heard the news, I was hoping you'd change your mind. I'm sorry that you're coming on under these circumstances, but we'll both forget about that soon enough. In a week you'll be working so hard you won't remember *what* happened. I'm very, very pleased, Jen. For Eton as well as for myself."

Jennifer smiled. "Good," she said. "I am too."

"And Jennifer, I think we should get something

straight before you start—before you even come in to firm up the final details."

"What's that?" she asked.

"I want to know what's bothering you," he said softly. "Or what was bothering you the other evening. You were so silent, so suddenly somewhere else. I want to know what it was about."

Jennifer hesitated. Wasn't it all moot now anyway, now that she'd be working with Joe? "Oh, it was nothing, really," she said. "I was just tired of your asking me to join you at Eton, I suppose. At the time I thought it was silly to keep talking about."

"I'm glad it paid off," he said. "How about dinner to celebrate? I'm not finishing up here till eight or so, but we could grab a late bite."

"I don't think so," she said carefully. She wanted to bring up the fact that if she were going to be working at Eton, she wanted more than ever to keep the relationship on a professional level. But he probably understood that; and perhaps she would look like a fool for bringing up something he had probably forgotten about. "I'm going to have a lot of loose ends to tie up at Civette, Joe. I haven't even told them I'm leaving, and—"

"And you're not going to eat between now and then?"

She laughed. "Well . . ."

"Well, indeed. I can take a hint. Look. Call me or my secretary at the office to set up a time when we can firm up the details. And I'll see you then, all right?"

"Okay, Joe. Good-bye." She hung up, wondering whether she had once again taken the easy road, done what she always had by saying no and narrowing her life.

Despite the awkwardness she had felt during that first phone call, Jennifer found her move to Eton a week later to be remarkably painless. Her office was lovely, just down the hall from Joe's, and overlooking Central Park. It was decorated very much like her apartment, in soft shades of slate blue and off-white. Her staff—a secretary and two assistants—was friendly, if a bit disorganized, having been without a director for weeks. And the press release on her appointment, which Joe had written himself, was glowing and almost embarrassingly enthusiastic.

Joe was true to his promise, too, that after a week Jennifer would be working so hard she'd forget the pressures under which she had been virtually forced to work at Eton. The first major order of business—organizing and ordering new market-research campaigns for five new product ideas—took up so much time that it seemed to Jennifer as if all she did was work, eat, and sleep in an endless and tiring cycle of days and nights.

Joe apparently sensed her wishes, too, about maintaining the relationship as a professional one. True, he often played games—holding her gaze too long, brushing up against her, communicating deeply and thoroughly that his thoughts, along with hers, dwelled endlessly on their past lovemaking; but for the most part, he was so busy dealing with problems at the new factory out in Fort Worth that he and Jennifer hardly saw each other.

After Jennifer had been at Eton for two weeks, Joe

90

asked her to stop by his office before the day was through. When she walked down the long hall toward his office a bit before five, she smiled to herself, remembering that other walk down a long hall toward Joe's office at Essences. She had come a long way.

When Jennifer went in, she was shocked by Joe's appearance. She hadn't seen him in the past few days, and he looked tired to the point of exhaustion, his face thinner than usual and his eyes heavy with fatigue.

"Come on in and sit down," he said quietly, barely looking up.

She sat on the couch, and he came out from behind his desk and sat next to her. "I need your help," he said in a near-whisper.

She looked at him with concern. "Of course. What's the matter?"

He rubbed the bridge of his nose and then brushed his hair back from his forehead. "I'm feeling rather beleaguered at the moment, Jen. I'm so exhausted from the Fort Worth business that I don't even know if I make any sense." He sighed. "But I feel the company's going in the wrong direction, as if we'll never make it if we keep doing what we're doing. The board of directors is having fits over our third-quarter net income, our R&D people aren't coming up with anything new." He shrugged. "I'm beginning to think it's one big waste of time, unless we can come up with something great."

"We can try," Jennifer put in hopefully.

"I want to do more than try," he said almost roughly. "We're stagnating. Everyone in this industry is. We're all putting out the same damn products in different packaging with different advertising. I want Eton to come up with something people will love." He sighed and shook his head. "Maybe I'm dreaming. I just feel . . . under a lot of pressure, I suppose." He looked into her eyes. "I guess I want to know someone's really with me in all of this. Really behind me." He paused. "I want that someone to be you, Jen."

"I—I'm with you," she murmured.

He cupped her face in his hands and searched the depths of her eyes. Her breath quickened. "Come to me," he said quietly, and her eyes closed as she pulled him close, and her fingers found the luxuriant softness of his hair. "I've missed you so," he sighed. With a moan he pressed his lips to hers. She answered with the parting of her lips, the play of her tongue with his, the beating of her heart as she held him close.

He pulled his head back. "You're an inspiration to me," he murmured. "Thank God you're here."

"Oh, Joe, I shouldn't be," she whispered.

"Why not? This is as it should be, as it should always have been."

"It can't be," she murmured, her lips in his hair, against his ear, along his neck. She wanted to believe her own words, to put some force or an ounce of conviction behind them. "Remember what I said," she whispered right before his lips claimed hers again, sending an urgent message of liquid desire flowing through her body. She moaned and held him closer, wanting to feel the pressure of his chest against her breasts, aching to feel him even closer to her, her body arching in search of his.

His hand was on her thigh then, and with his searing touch he awakened every part of her body in a coursing spiral of warmth. He began to move it up, igniting each inch of flesh as it edged upward.

She tore her mouth from his. This was the last chance, the last moment before it would be too late.

"Come home with me," he urged. "Come home and make love with me, Jennifer. Come alive for me as you were meant to. Love me," he whispered into her ear.

She closed her eyes. It was so hard to say no. But she simply had to. He aroused her as no one else ever had, stirred feelings and emotions and sensations she had never felt before. It was a door she wasn't ready to open, a place she wasn't ready to go. "I just can't," she murmured, opening her eyes.

He was looking at her with a mixture of tension and understanding. He laughed humorlessly. "You're so worried about our relationship, Jennifer, but *I* may be the one to quit at this rate." Then he smiled. "It's going to be extremely difficult if we keep this up, you know." He shook his head. "I wouldn't want you to stop working here—I wouldn't change it—but God, I wish you'd change your mind, Jen."

"So do I," she murmured. "I wish I could be . . . freer, or less worried about the future. But the time just isn't right." She didn't want to go into the details, the images she had of how difficult it would be to come in to work if they had had a fight, if Joe were with another woman, if things simply didn't work out. She couldn't open herself up to that possi-

93

bility, not at this point in her life. Yet she knew that mixing her work and this relationship was not the primary problem. The problem lay within her, wrapped in a tremendous fear of losing Joe and whatever he felt for her at that moment. She knew he was fond of her—he liked her, he needed her, he wanted to make love with her—and though she kept herself at a distance from all those pleasures, that distance was better than the possibility of losing them forever.

The phone rang, and Joe jumped. He was obviously still tense over his worries. "Excuse me," he said, and stood and strode over to his desk. "Yes? . . . What? Yes, hold on." He turned to Jennifer. "It's the switchboard. You've got a call and she wants to know if you'll take it in here."

Jennifer frowned and stood up. "Sure," she said. "It's probably DataCom."

Joe handed her the phone, and she watched as he walked away. He ran a hand through his hair—a gesture she realized was something he did when he was tired, perhaps annoyed—and went over to the window, where he stood gazing out over the evening skyline. "Hello?" Jennifer said. No answer. "Hello?" she repeated.

"Jennifer?" came a female voice, a near-whisper.

"Who's this?"

"Caroline," the voice hissed. "Listen. Are you in Mr. Brennan's office or what?"

"Yes, I am. Why are you whispering? What's the matter?"

"Damn. I didn't want to call you *there* of all places."

"Caroline, what's the matter? If—"

94

"Shh," Caroline cut in. "I don't want him to know there's anything wrong. Just listen and try not to say anything, okay?"

"Okay, then shoot."

"Listen, Jennifer. I don't know if you've noticed or not, but I haven't exactly been Miss Attendance of the Year at Eton the past two weeks."

"Well, I hadn't seen—"

"Please, Jennifer. Don't say anything. That Joe Brennan has ears where most people have a heart. Listen. All I want to know is, has he said anything to you about me? I mean lately?"

"No," Jennifer answered. She wanted to say more, to ask Caroline why she hadn't been coming in. Caroline sounded worried. Well, she'd say something even if Caroline *did* mind; she still felt somewhat responsible for her cousin. "Are you all right, hon? What's—"

"Please, Jennifer. It's nothing. Don't even ask. I just haven't been able to face going in, and Tim had some time off, so . . . I know it's bad, and I'm really going to try from now on. But I wanted to be sure I wasn't about to get the ax before I made my big improvement."

"Well, nothing's going on that I know of," Jennifer said. Out of the corner of her eye she saw Joe turn around. She turned away, wanting to concentrate only on the conversation.

"All right," Caroline breathed. "But listen. I know you're not on such great terms with Joe Brennan yourself, but if you hear anything I should know, give me a buzz right away, okay? Oh, there's Tim. I've got to go."

"Okay, hon. Bye."

When Jennifer turned around, Joe was looking at her with concern. "What's the matter?" he asked.

"Oh, nothing," Jennifer said absently, still thinking about Caroline. She didn't like the sound of Caroline's voice. There was a fear there, an evasiveness that made her nervous.

"Nothing?" Joe came toward the desk, planted his palms on its surface, and looked into Jennifer's eyes. "Your cousin calls you in a panicked voice, you have a conversation that's obviously designed to prevent anyone else from knowing what it's about, and you say nothing. Why did you ask her if she was all right then?"

Jennifer raised her chin. "For your information, Joe, she's my cousin, and from time to time we do ask each other how we are."

"Not in that tone of voice you don't. Damn it, Jennifer, if there's trouble, I want to help. Why can't you accept that?"

"It's a family matter," she returned quietly. "Why can't you accept *that*?"

His eyes darkened as they gazed into hers, as if he could read her thoughts. "It has to do with Eton, doesn't it," he said quietly. It was a statement rather than a question.

She willed herself not to let her expression change. "I don't know why you say that," she said hollowly.

His features softened. "Because I know you, Jen," he said gently. "Look at me."

She did, though it was difficult, almost painful, as she gazed into a look of deep concern, deep caring.

"What is Caroline worried about?" he asked.

Jennifer's eyes widened. The question wasn't at all what she had expected, and Joe had used an almost prosecutorial tone of voice. "What do you think you're doing? This isn't a courtroom."

"I want to know what's going on."

"Why?" she demanded. "Because you care or because you think it has something to do with the damn company? I wonder—if you knew it had nothing to do with Eton, would you be so concerned?"

"That's not fair," he said, swinging a hip onto the desk. "I can't help but care about Eton, Jennifer. But I care about you too."

She sighed and closed her eyes. What had she just said? Why was she flying off the handle like this? She shook her head and opened her eyes. "Look. I'm sorry. I don't know what got into me. I guess I'm a little concerned about Caroline. She's kind of like the little sister I never had, and I'm a little overprotective of her. Anyway, I'm sorry. I know that . . . that you care."

He sighed. "Good. And you know what's bothering you, don't you?"

She looked at him without answering. His eyes were a blue version of what she knew her own eyes were: full of longing and regret, acceptance and resignation.

"I'll respect your wishes," he said quietly. "But it won't be easy."

SIX

Over the next few weeks Jennifer thought often of Joe's words to her that day in his office. He had promised he'd respect her wishes. Yet all she ever felt when she thought of those words was doubt and anger.

She had closed herself off once again from what might have been a satisfying relationship, an action that guaranteed she wouldn't be hurt; but how would she gain that way? How would she ever grow close to anyone?

When she looked back on her affair with Andrew Cole, she wondered whether it had been more important than she had thought in the development of her wariness and mistrust, her willingness to cut herself off from others in the interest of emotional safety. She remembered the lovemaking—tense and faltering, passionless and dry. She had thought there was something wrong with her—emotionally or physically or both—and had been depressed and anxious for weeks. Yet she had been unwilling to discuss the problem with Andrew, who didn't seem to notice anything was even wrong. And then one day she realized—so clearly she must have known deep down all the time—there was nothing wrong with her; her unwillingness to discuss her feelings with Andrew was just one of many symptoms that added up to one big fact: She didn't love him. She simply didn't love him.

The revelation was eye-opening, more liberating than sad at first, for she had been feeling so unhappy, unfulfilled, and unloved before. But soon afterward Jennifer had closed herself off more than ever, without even realizing it. Since then she had had to force herself to give people a second chance—even a second look—and on a deep level, she had unconsciously decided that she wasn't made for love, that it simply wasn't in the cards.

Yet lately small patches of easy pleasure and openness had shone on her days like light coming through a forest. As she looked back she could remember so many moments with Joe—shared laughter, shared thoughts, looks exchanged during meetings, feelings she knew they shared. And she felt as if she were melting, slowly, like ice in the warm sun.

Joe had been true to his word too. Though his blue eyes caught her sometimes in gazes so thick with meaning she lost her voice, he never touched her—or no more than she touched him. By accident. When they were alone in a room together, usually his office, though he seemed to be stopping by hers almost every morning—they kept their distances, their tacit agreement underlying every glance and pause. As difficult as his eyes were to resist, his voice was more so. It became husky and edged with desire when he was with her, and the ragged hoarseness touched her physically, warmed her body with a glow of desire.

And she saw that she was melting, letting him closer each time they touched—emotionally, physically, in their thoughts, in their dreams.

And one day, when Jennifer had been at Eton almost a month, she saw that she suddenly seemed to be Joe's only true ally at Eton. She had been so caught up in her work that she simply hadn't noticed she and Joe had become isolated from everyone else at the company, as if on an island of their own.

Joe had a lot of support from the less well-paid employees at Eton—the secretaries and assistants, mostly—but among most department heads, he was resented, unreasonably, Jennifer felt, for constantly demanding more from them: more time, more ideas, more enthusiasm, more commitment. Jennifer had never seen such an uncooperative group at that corporate level, but knew the situation was common whenever someone new took over a company. And she also suspected, since virtually all of the department heads were male, that personality conflicts were responsible for a good part of the trouble.

Joe might have been better able to stem the loss of support for his tenure had it not been for occasional slaps in the face from totally unexpected quarters: one of the main trade papers, *Cosmetics News*. A few weeks earlier a small item had said that Joe had bought tickets for all his employees to attend the Fragrance and Cosmetics Institute's Annual Charity

Ball "in a last-ditch attempt to bolster plummeting employee morale, at a company whose pre-tax profits are plummeting as well." While the item was true, it had served only to make matters worse.

A second item, appearing only a week later, had been part of an article about the stock market. It had said:

> The firing of Thorpe/McKay/Kendall as Eton's agency is, according to our sources, the first of many steps planned by pres. Joe Brennan to pull ailing Eton up by its bootstraps. Says one Wall Street analyst, 'Our buyers get jittery when they hear of moves like this. Joe Brennan should map out a solid plan of action instead of waffling as he's done so far. Investors are willing to hop along with a company like that only just so far.'

The item, once again, had been essentially true, but it had created just one more negative image Joe had had to fight.

Jennifer wanted to help Joe, but she knew the best way for her to do that was to be as effective in her job as she could. Her assistants were among Joe's most loyal supporters, so together they all formed a strong bloc that could do much for Joe and Eton.

And today, exactly one month since she had begun at Eton, she had just finished drafting plans for a new line of products that could possibly be Eton's ticket out of its slump.

When she went into Joe's office, he was on the phone, but he waved her in and continued talking. "No, Jim. Listen. I don't care. . . . Damn it, you put me in charge of the company, now give me some room. . . . No, no way. Give me room, Jim, or there's no point in my being here. . . . Yes, that's what that means. Please think about it."

He hung up, and when he looked up at Jennifer standing in front of the desk, he shook his head. "Now the board doesn't want us to go ahead with any new projects," he said, his voice edged with fatigue. "I told them—and they know—it's the only way out of the slump. But it's going to take some heavy convincing."

Jennifer sighed. "They have to believe you," she said.

"Not necessarily," he said, standing up. "It might be easier just to bring someone else in. It'd be cheaper than product-development costs."

"That's crazy. Whoever they got to replace you would be faced with the same problem."

"Don't look for logic, Jennifer, or ask for it in this business—in any business that's in trouble. The board is desperate, and they're terrified of losing more money. *You* know R&D costs are astronomical. They do have a point."

"Not against what we're coming up with," Jennifer said. "Here. I'll show you." She walked over to the couch and set her portfolio on the low table in front of it, and Joe sat down next to her. "I don't pretend all our troubles will be over," Jennifer said, spreading out her work, "but I think this could help."

When she glanced at him, her next words flew out of her mind—for he was looking at her with a look she had never seen—of awe mixed with confusion, as

102

if he were seeing her for the first time, and liking, or even loving, what he saw. Jennifer held his gaze, melting into his blue-gray look, wanting to melt into his arms.

She took a breath and cleared her throat. "Uh, anyway," she said vaguely. "Well. Maybe I should just . . . maybe you should look at this yourself," she began again, and hastily took out the proposal her secretary had typed that morning.

"Why don't you tell me about it?" he murmured.

"Well. All right," she answered, looking away. It was so difficult to talk, even to think, with Joe gazing at her as he was. "All right," she began. "As you'll see, if you look at this, it's a plan for a whole line of products geared to an older market than what we've gone after up to now. Part of this is based on recent research, part on my intuition, but we can back this up with more for the board. It will be a full line— skin care, shampoo, makeup, everything except perfume—and one of the points will be that it isn't sticky or overly scented or heavy. It's geared to health, and vitality, and spirit, for the active woman who wants a total beauty system that's actually good for her. All the products will be high in protein, low in dyes. And I thought we'd call them Amino-Actives—amino for the high protein level, actives to go along with the ad campaign, which will be geared to the athletic, aware woman. 'The woman who knows what she wants' could be one of our key phrases."

Joe smiled. "I like it. I like it a lot, Jen." He raised a brow. "Whether the board will is another matter though. We're not budgeted for a complete new line for another two years."

"To hell with the budget," Jennifer said. "I don't think we have a choice, Joe. They've got to remember that when you came on at Eton, the company was almost nothing, and you've got almost nothing to work with."

"It's wonderful to have you behind me like this, Jennifer. But I don't know if—"

"Just listen and look," she interrupted, taking out the rest of her presentation. She had worked late into the night at home for the past week, and had developed the presentation well beyond what was usually expected at this point, including rough storyboards —sketches with the planned voice-over—for future commercials.

They went over the storyboards and draft in detail. Joe had asked his secretary to hold all his calls until the meeting was over, and with the darkening sky churning before the thunderstorm that had been trying to break all day, the atmosphere was thick and heavy. Jennifer's attention was drawn away from the storyboards to the gentle coaxing of Joe's smooth voice, the gentle urging of his scent, the awareness in his eyes that matched her own. And she realized she was living something she had dreamed of—working with Joe, meeting him on equal terms, sharing an unspoken desire, laughing at unspoken fears. Yet it was much richer than she had imagined back then, for back then she had idolized Joe, put him on a pedestal so high she couldn't know him, or trust him, or . . . love him.

She looked at his handsome profile as he studied her work—long, dark lashes framing cerulean eyes, golden-brown hair tinged with gray at the temples, skin rough with whiskers she could feel just by looking.

It was silly to think about love though. After all, she had almost felt this way about Andrew Cole, hadn't she?

No, came a voice from somewhere deep within. Joe was smiling at that moment over something she had written, and when she saw that smile, she knew.

He shook his head, straightened out the layouts, and sighed. "You've done a beautiful job, Jennifer." He looked at her and frowned. "Everything I say seems to come out wrong, as if I'm praising you from on high. I don't mean it to sound that way." He reached out and brushed a strand of hair back from her forehead. "It's almost a matter of the two of us against everyone else now," he said, wrapping a curl of her hair in his fingers.

"That's not true," she protested. "You know you've got a lot of support—really loyal, enthusiastic support in my department, and almost everybody in the others. It's just the department heads you've got to worry about."

He gazed into her eyes. "That's not what I'm talking about," he said quietly. "I'm talking about you and me. You—a woman who understands everything I want, everything I need, without even being aware of how important you are. A woman whose eyes can make me forget all that I want to forget." He inhaled deeply, his eyes closing partway. "A woman I can't touch, except perhaps as I'm touching you now, because that's as you want it"—he paused —"and I want to please you in every way I can."

Jennifer's lips parted. "Joe, I—"

105

"Shh," he murmured, moving his index finger to her lips.

The touch was almost too much. Jennifer wanted to close her lips over his flesh, take his hand in hers and hold it close, take him in her arms. But she gently moved his hand away. She needed time to think, to—

"Jennifer."

Her eyes met his, and a flood of desire warmed her. "Yes," she murmured.

His lips curved into a slow smile. "I think we have something to celebrate tonight, don't you?" His smile was gentle yet knowing.

"I . . . guess we do," she said dreamily. Her emotions were shifting, whirling, coalescing.

"I'll pick you up at your place? Eight o'clock?"

He held her with his eyes, and she said yes.

Jennifer's whole body was alive with sensation, coursing with an electricity that was thrilling. As she pulled her sheer cotton dress over her head and let it slip softly around her, every spot the smooth material touched was awakened, aroused as if by Joe's very touch. She wasn't going to try to analyze her feelings, to take them apart and examine them, or to hide from them either. All she knew—all she wanted to know—was that every inch of her body felt alive and tingling with excitement, and she simply wasn't going to fight anymore.

And she saw, as she looked in the mirror, that there was no way she could hide her feelings either. Though she had had approximately two nights' sleep over the past week, her eyes were shining and glowing with an inner vitality that had somehow gotten rid of the circles under her eyes. Her quickened pulse made her skin glow smooth and pink at the mere thought of Joe.

Jennifer put on almost no makeup. She had showered and washed and dried her hair before getting dressed, and now, as she looked into the mirror, she decided to let her old makeup routine fall by the wayside along with her fears and worries. She looked good—with a little eyeliner and a touch of lipstick she'd look great—and to hell with what she usually did.

A few minutes before Joe was due to arrive the phone rang. It was Caroline, wanting to know if she could come over for dinner the next night.

"Of course," Jennifer agreed. Since Caroline's worried phone call at Joe's office a few weeks earlier, Jennifer hadn't been able to get any more information from her other than that things were "better." It would be good to have a chance to sit and talk and let Caroline unburden herself if she wanted to. "Why don't you come by my office when you're finished up, or a little after five if you can stand it—and we can come back here together."

"Okay," Caroline said. "It'll probably do you some good getting out of that office anyway. You've been working like a dog."

"There's a lot to be done," Jennifer said.

"Well, that's not what *I* hear."

"What do you mean?" Jennifer asked.

"Everyone's saying that you and Joe Brennan are having an affair. I mean, some people are. *I* know you're not, and who cares anyway except that he's a

107

bastard, but I've tried to set as many people straight as I could."

Jennifer gave a little laugh. "How many people are you talking about? It sounds like a cast of thousands."

"Oh, you know how it is. What else is there to talk about, especially when you've got two people who are good-looking and together all the time?"

Jennifer was about to reply when the doorbell rang. "Oh. Listen. There's the bell. I'll see you tomorrow, hon."

"Okay, Jennifer. Hey, anyone I know?"

"No," Jennifer lied. "See you tomorrow."

She hung up, took a quick look in the foyer mirror, and walked to the door. Caroline's call bothered her a bit, but when she opened the door and saw Joe standing there she forgot all about it.

It was obvious from his eyes that her efforts in looking good hadn't been wasted. He stood gazing at her from head to toe, his eyes dark with appreciation, his mouth pursed in a half smile. "Well. I had wondered why I had let you go. But it was worth the wait. You look beautiful, Jennifer." He shook his head. "Just beautiful."

She smiled. "Thanks. Come on in."

A few moments later, sitting on the couch in the living room, Jennifer and Joe were raising glasses of rich red wine in a toast.

"To second chances," he said softly. "Even when they're years later." He raised a brow. "And to your new idea, naturally," he added. "May it save Eton from otherwise certain disaster."

She smiled, and they drank, looking into each other's eyes.

"You know," she said, "a lot of people at Eton seem to be less concerned with the company's success than with whether you and I are sleeping together. I just spoke to Caroline and she asked me whether we were."

The hint of a smile appeared. "Does that bother you?" he asked.

"A little. Not as much as I would have thought."

He raised a brow. "You're not worried people will think you got where you are by sleeping with the boss?"

She shrugged. "You and I know that isn't true."

Looking deeply into her eyes, he reached forward and took her hand in his. "I know that I want you," he said, his voice deep with desire. He brought her hand up to the base of his throat, where she could feel his heart pounding. "You can feel it here," he whispered. "And here," he said, bringing her hand down to his chest, placing it over the fabric covering his left nipple. She felt it rise under her touch—a touch she hadn't even meant to give—and looked into his eyes. "What about you?" he murmured. He uncovered her hand and gently touched the soft skin of her neck, its pulse equaling his. "I want to know," he whispered, and his hands roved downward, tracing her tingling nipples lightly, edging inside her dress—between the buttons—and heating her flesh.

Her eyes closed under the touch, and then his lips were on hers, and she sank back into the softness of the couch under his lean frame, his hard thighs touching hers in a way she had dreamed of long, long ago.

He raised his head and looked into her eyes. "I want to know everything about you," he said huskily, raising himself to the side and running a hand down along the front of her dress, between her breasts and downward. "I want to know every touch that pleases you, everything you crave." His hand kneaded her hip, her thigh, sending shimmering paths of heat beyond, awakening a desire that took her breath away. He found the bottom edge of her dress and brought it up, and then his hand was touching the warm flesh of her thigh, and she moaned in need. "Oh, Joe," she cried.

"I want to know you want me," he said, edging hot circles along her fiery skin. "I want to know you need me," he rasped, "as much as I need you."

"Yes," she moaned, as his hand moved upward, finding the edge of her bikini. She arched herself in desire, and he agonizingly trailed his hand away.

He braced himself against the edge of the couch and looked down into her eyes. "Jennifer, I don't think I've ever wanted a woman as much as I want you. I want to know every inch of your body and please you more than you've ever dreamed. But I want to be sure it's right for you." Again, he reached his hand under her dress and lightly brought it upward, tracing over the gentle rise of her stomach. "I want to see you," he murmured. "Now, as you're wanting me."

"Please," she whispered, her voice heavy with desire. As he slid his hands underneath her, she raised herself up, and he pulled her dress over her head and then slid her underpants off. She lay naked beside him, and as his ardent gaze roved over her she whispered, "I was made for you." With a groan he closed his eyes and brought his thigh around her, making her tremble with need.

"I want to feel your skin against mine, Joe," she whispered hoarsely, eyes half-closed in desire. He took her in his arms then, kissing her deeply, and then looked into her eyes. "God, how wonderful you are."

When he got off the couch to undress, Jennifer stretched lazily and watched him. He was mesmerizing, handsomer than she had imagined, his broad chest well-muscled and firm, his thighs lean and hard.

And then he was beside her, gazing into her eyes with fire and excitement and desire, a warm arm along her hips, a possessive hand on her thigh. "I could look at you like this forever," he said softly. "and I could hold you in my arms forever." Gently his fingers stroked the curve of her inner thigh, moving higher and higher until Jennifer was filled with a surging need, a shimmering desire that putting her arms around him wouldn't satisfy. She raked a hand along his back, along his buttocks, but she wanted him closer, close enough to satisfy the smoldering yearning that was washing through her.

Gently he rolled her over onto her back, and gazed down at her with breathless pleasure. He inhaled deeply and slid a firm thigh over hers, and she moaned and pulled him closer.

"You *were* made for me, Jen," he whispered, moving on top of her. "And I for you."

"Oh Joe," she said hoarsely. "I need you."

He urged a thigh between her legs and placed a hand of fire underneath her. Every inch of his hard body was insistent and coaxing, melting her into simmering desire that spread through her in pulsing waves of need, aching waves of enveloping fervor.

"Then I'm yours," he rasped, and with a blazing surge that made her cry out his name and cling to him, he took her beyond desire into pleasure that kept growing, surging, spiraling as he urged her on, cried her name, gently bit her shoulders, her neck, her lips. "We were made for each other, Jen," he moaned, "meant for this always."

"Yes," she answered breathlessly. "Oh, yes."

And they clung to each other urgently as their passion flamed into shimmering release, cries of ecstasy uniting them, and then gently slowing, swirling downward, until they lay together in wondrous contentment.

Jennifer sighed happily and let her cheek rest on Joe's chest. She loved the feel of it—damp from their lovemaking, scratchy with hair. "I love you," she said dreamily, brushing her lips against a nipple and settling in more comfortably. Her eyelids succumbed to their weight, and closed.

His hand gently squeezed her shoulder, and he rested his chin against the top of her head, and she felt the rise and fall of his chest as he sighed.

He stroked her hair gently and slowly, as if he were not conscious that he was doing so, and Jennifer began to ebb off into a dreamy half sleep, when her eyes flew open. What had she just murmured? "I love you." And what had he replied? Nothing. God! How could she have let herself go like that?

Without realizing it she dug her fingers into his chest.

"Whoa!" he cried. "Jennifer. What's wrong?"

She rose up on one elbow and looked into his eyes. But it was painful to do so, for his eyes were questioning, apologetic, asking forgiveness. She looked away. "Sorry if I hurt you," she said, and lay her head against his chest again.

She had made a mistake. She could feel it in every inch of her body. Beyond the level of dos and don'ts she had read and hated in magazines for years ("*Never* say 'I love you' unless he says it first"), she could feel that she had frightened him, and that something had just flown from the relationship, never to return. During their lovemaking she had felt loved—loved as she had never felt in her life, loved with a strength that amazed her. Joe's passion had seemed of two parts—joy in loving, joy in being loved, as if he, too, had been hungry as she was, as he had never realized.

For a painful moment she remembered making love with Andrew Cole. His actions had seemed clinically determined, as if he were following an instruction book. Being with Andrew hadn't, in fact, been making love; it had been having sex.

But Joe—every movement of his, every touch, every kiss, every whispered urging word—had been filled with love, a desire to please and be pleased, a tenderness that transcended even his most ardent movements, his most fevered touches. And his actions, his cries of "Jennifer," his deep kisses at the most exquisitely exciting of moments, had communicated deeply into her very soul—love.

And without thinking she had voiced her feelings easily, at what had obviously been the wrong time. And she had learned something she hadn't even wanted to wonder about either way: He didn't love her.

It was the first time she had ever told a man she loved him.

She wished she had said nothing, or that she could explain. *I've never felt this way before, I've never felt this loved before, and I thought* . . . But, no. She had said enough already.

Perhaps if she kept her eyes closed and concentrated on the warm feel of his arms around her, the gentle rise and fall of his chest, the feel of his skin against hers . . . perhaps she could recapture the feeling.

SEVEN

The next afternoon, though Jennifer hadn't been looking forward to it, she was actually relieved Caroline was going to meet her at the office and go home with her for dinner. She would have been grateful, she realized, for virtually anyone or anything to take her mind off Joe.

She was angry at herself as well as at him, and the anger was made more painful by the fact that she knew neither she nor he had actually done anything wrong. She had opened herself up to an experience she had never had, allowing herself to be reached for the first time by another human being. He had touched her soul, awakened her as no one else ever had. And she had responded quite naturally, but as naively as a child.

And today he had acted as if none of it had ever happened. Jennifer could hardly bear to think about it, but the incident kept replaying itself in her mind, never fading, never even becoming any less detailed.

That morning, she had gone into Joe's office, perhaps foolishly, she now realized, for she had gone in only to say hello, to be with him, without knowing if he was busy or not. She had sailed in, but she saw his secretary, Laura, sitting in front of his desk hurriedly writing on a steno pad, and had become instantly and completely self-conscious. She muttered something about talking to Joe later about a "marketing concept," and Joe, smiling, had casually dismissed his secretary.

When Laura had left, Joe looked at Jennifer with bemusement. "You were saying?" he said, leaning back and lacing his fingers behind his head.

"I—" She had been planning to laugh, perhaps to share a joke about the "marketing concept" that didn't exist, to switch gears and return to last night the minute Laura had left. But apparently Joe was perfectly comfortable acting, in the office, at least, as if they were merely colleagues. She was ready to do the same, naturally. She didn't plan to have her arms around him twenty-four hours a day, but it was a shock to begin without one word—*nothing*—about last night.

"I, uh, wanted to talk to you about an idea I had," she said, hoping he couldn't read her feelings. "But I don't think now is quite the right time," she said. "I'd . . . rather think about it a bit more fully."

He tilted his head and looked at her with pleasure. "Whatever you say," he said. He raised a brow. "Is that all?"

"Yes, I'll see you later," she said, and hastily

116

looked at her watch. "I have a meeting I'm late for," she murmured, and turned and left his office.

Now, as she thought about the incident, she wished she had been more self-possessed, more sure of herself. And she didn't want to think about what the incident meant in terms of Joe and his feelings. Could she have been so wrong about him, so blinded by some need, that she had misread him completely? As things stood now Joe seemed perfectly content to treat the night before as a self-contained incident rather than a beginning. And then she remembered his words: *I wouldn't want to see you turn down a wonderful opportunity because of something that might not work out.* God. Was this what he had had in mind?

She took a deep breath to try to slow down the pounding of her heart. A moment later Caroline came bursting in to Jennifer's office, as cheerful as always.

Having Caroline over for dinner turned out to be the welcome diversion Jennifer had hoped it would be. They made a mess of the kitchen, making delicious chili and biscuits, and they both drank too much beer.

But toward the end of dinner Caroline grew serious the moment Jennifer mentioned Eton. Sitting across from Jennifer on one of the living room couches, she took a big sip of beer and looked at Jennifer almost fearfully. "I don't want to talk about work, okay?"

Jennifer sighed. "No, it's not okay. Give me at least a few minutes. I haven't been able to talk to you

117

since you called me at Joe's office that afternoon, and I'd really like to know what's going on. Maybe I can help."

Caroline looked at her skeptically. "I don't think so," she said quietly, her voice low and on the verge of tears.

Jennifer frowned. "Caroline, what's the matter? Please tell me."

Caroline quickly shook her head. "Uh-uh. I can't. I mean, it's nothing." She tried to smile. "And I've been pretty good lately attendancewise, so . . ." Her voice trailed off. "It doesn't matter anyway," she said vaguely. "I don't think I'll be there much longer." She narrowed her eyes at Jennifer. "Say, listen, Jennifer. Maybe it's none of my business, but are you having an affair with Joe Brennan or not?"

Jennifer blinked. "Why do you ask?"

Caroline widened her eyes. "Well, I *told* you that everyone thinks so, and if it's true, I don't feel like being the last to know. I mean, I had thought you couldn't stand the guy. All that revenge stuff and everything."

Jennifer managed to smile in an attempt to mask her feelings; she didn't even know what her relationship with Joe was at this point. "As far as I'm concerned, Caroline, it's nobody's business what my relationship is with Joe. I'd tell *you,* of course, but tonight isn't the night to ask." She shook her head. "But I'm definitely *not* out for revenge, if that's what you're asking. You must know that. I've been working very, very hard, and I'm really pleased with Joe as a . . . as a colleague."

118

Caroline took another hasty sip of beer. "Are you serious?"

Jennifer stared. "Of course. He's more than I expected. Much more. I think he's wonderful."

"Well, I don't," Caroline said. "He's a bastard."

Jennifer tilted her head. "To you? Because if he is, Caroline, I might be able to help. You asked me once before, and—"

Caroline shook her head. "Uh-uh. Just forget it, okay? If I'm not going to be there much longer, it's just silly for you to say anything." Her tone was uncharacteristically firm. "I really want you to stay out of it, okay?"

Jennifer shrugged. "Okay. Fine. But if you need my help, just let me know."

Caroline opened her mouth to say something but then changed her mind. Yet, when Jennifer looked into her eyes, the message was as clear as if Caroline had put it into words. She was in trouble of some sort.

The next morning Jennifer walked briskly down the corridor to her office, as if the day were a normal day and she hadn't spent a nearly sleepless night thinking about Joe. *Damn,* she thought. *Here I am in the very situation I had hoped to avoid—working with a man in a relationship I don't understand, at a job I might have to leave if things get difficult enough.* But as she walked into her office—a large room she had made very much her own—she was suddenly filled with determination. No matter what, she wouldn't quit the job because of Joe—no matter how awkward it became.

The buzzer on her intercom interrupted her thoughts. It was Sherry, her secretary, whispering that Joe Brennan was coming in, as at that moment he did, and that he looked very angry.

He strode in and was seated on the couch across from Jennifer's desk before Jennifer had even replaced the receiver. Jennifer was surprised to see, however, that he didn't look angry, merely concerned or perturbed, with his brows knit and his lips set in a frown.

When their eyes met she fought the impulse to soften, to melt under his gaze. She took a deep breath and looked at him questioningly. "Is there something wrong, Joe?" she said calmly.

He sighed angrily. "Yes, goddamn it, and if you'd stop hiding behind that desk and come over and sit with me instead, perhaps we could take a stab at working it out."

She rose from her chair. "I wasn't aware that sitting at one's desk is considered hiding. Remind me to mention that the next time I'm with one of the board members."

He didn't smile. "I don't really give a damn where you sit, as a matter of fact," he stated, his voice low and grating, "as long as you're honest with me."

She swallowed. He sounded very upset. "About what?" she asked, her voice annoyingly tinged with doubt.

"About yesterday," he said, standing up. He walked slowly over to her desk, his eyes never leaving hers, and hitched a hip over the edge on her side of the desk. He was sitting quite close, his lean thighs only inches from her, and she became angrier still.

"I don't know what you're referring to," she said coldly. "If you're talking about the new marketing concept, I told you—"

"You told me a lie," he cut in.

She couldn't look into his eyes. "What are you talking about?" she asked quietly.

He took a deep breath. "I'm talking," he began, "about something I consider very, very important." He paused. "I'm talking about us, and our roles in the office, and what I think was something of a misunderstanding on your part."

She looked into his eyes, but saw no clue as to what he was going to say. Her heart was racing. Were things even worse than she had imagined? Had people been gossiping more than usual about her and Joe? Joe had said he didn't care about things of that sort, but you could never really tell. . . .

Joe sighed. "When you left my office yesterday, you seemed upset. Rigid. Very much *unlike* the Jennifer I had come to know." He shrugged. "Since I hadn't done or said anything I thought could be the cause, I assumed you were upset about something that had nothing to do with me. Contrary to popular belief"—he smiled—"I do not believe the earth revolves around me. But I began to wonder. The whole incident bothered me." He frowned. "You hadn't mentioned a thing about the night before"—she could feel the color beginning to stain her cheeks—"and then all of a sudden I realized. Perhaps I had put you off." His eyes held hers and asked the silent question, *Is that it?*, and waited for her answer.

She looked away, feeling awkward and mistrustful.

"Jennifer," he said softly. "When you come on so strong in your work, it's very easy to forget that there's a person under there who doesn't know all the answers." She met his gaze. "Don't you think this needs some talking out, Jen? I don't think I can handle having you totally assertive about business and then so guarded about your feelings that it's impossible to get through to you—if we're going to be seeing each other, that is."

"All right," she breathed. "Look. You're right. I feel as if I'm walking on thin ice every time something or someone gets personal. But you're playing a little game of your own, in case you hadn't noticed."

"What's that?" he asked.

"You're as indefinite and vague as I am guarded. Everything you say is put in terms of 'if we're going to have a relationship,' or 'it may or may not work out.' I'm not cautious *because* of you, God knows, but it doesn't help that we're both totally indefinite!"

He raised his brows and started to smile, as did she, and then they were both laughing.

Joe shook his head. "You know what?"

"What?" she laughed.

"You're absolutely right. So. What's today?"

"Uh, May sixteenth."

"Great. Okay. Will you or will you not, Jennifer Preston, be the one and only, official and unofficial girl friend of one Joseph Brennan, i.e., me."

She laughed. "Yes," she answered without hesitation.

He winked. "Great. Then we're an item—no ifs,

122

ands, or buts about it—and May sixteenth is our official anniversary."

She laughed. "Okay, great."

"Good. Now that that's settled, Jennifer, let's get back to business."

And for the next half hour, laughing half the time and being serious the rest, they did get back to business. Joe said it was too soon to tell whether the Ardence campaign was a success or not, but the board of directors had liked it and had requested a public-relations campaign that would, as they had put it, "interface with the existing marketing campaign."

"I'd like to *interface* their jargon-ridden butts," Joe muttered. "But in the meantime, Jen, I need something good and something fast." He smiled in challenge. "Like that new 'marketing concept' you told me about yesterday."

Jennifer glared at him. "Drop it, or else. And yes to the campaign. I actually *have* been playing around with an idea for Ardence. But I have to let it simmer a little bit before I figure out what it is."

He looked at her doubtfully. "Sounds mysterious, possibly, but not *necessarily* interesting. My really good ideas always come to me in a flash."

"Which is why you hired me, so they can be more than half-baked." She smiled. "Now, leave me alone so I can work this out. I may even have something for you tomorrow."

Joe shook his head. "And I thought that underneath it all you were such a romantic. Our anniversary and I don't even get a kiss?"

She stood up. "Mmm. Sounds nice." And he stood and took her in his arms, and as his lips brushed hers lightly, then claimed them in a long, deep kiss, Jennifer lazily realized she had never been happier.

EIGHT

After Joe left, Jennifer asked Sherry to hold all calls
except from Joe, and settled in to spend the rest of
the afternoon working on her idea for Ardence. A bit
before five a harried Sherry said Jennifer's cousin had
called four times, and could she possibly speak to
her.

Jennifer said yes, and moments later Caroline was
on the line. "Jennifer, listen. I know you were kind
of vague and all about you and Joe, but I want you
to do me a gigantic favor anyway. See what you
think."

"What is it?"

"Well. It doesn't matter if you and Joe are really
going out together or not. The point is that you work
together and you hang around together, and I
thought . . . Well, I thought maybe you and Joe could
double date with me and Tim."

Jennifer smiled. It was odd hearing Caroline use

such an old-fashioned term. "I'd love to, Caroline, but I'd have to ask Joe."

"Listen. It would be a big favor. I mean, Tim doesn't know too many people. I don't know, he just doesn't seem to have that many friends. And you know *I* don't yet, so—"

"You don't have to make excuses, hon. It sounds nice. I'll let you know." After discussing the details, Jennifer hung up and dialed Joe's extension.

She still had a smile on her face as she dialed, and wondered whether she had been smiling most of the afternoon. She felt carefree, competent, and wonderful in the most simple of ways.

Joe was happy to hear from her, but as soon as she mentioned the double date, there was a silence.

"Joe?"

"I'm here." He paused. "Jen, I don't think we should spend our time arguing over something as unimportant as this, but going out with your cousin, whom I like well enough, and Tim Somers, whom I don't, is not the kind of evening I had in mind for when we next get together."

"It doesn't have to be our next time, Joe. That's Saturday. This is only Wednesday."

He sighed. "All right. So what are you doing tonight?"

"Let's see. I have aerobics class from eight to ten, but then I'm free."

"At ten? I'm dying to see you, but I do need *some* sleep."

"Well, what about tomorrow?" she asked.

"Can't do. Jerry Loomis is coming in from Fort

126

Worth, and we're meeting day and night. What about Friday?"

"Nope," she said. "I've got class at the Alliance Française."

He sighed. "I always knew you'd be a stubborn pain in the butt, Jen. Okay, Saturday then. If I have to see you with Tim and Caroline to see you at all, I will."

"Great. I'll make the arrangements then."

"Jennifer."

She could hear him smiling. "Yes, Joe."

"This relationship is never going to work if we keep it up at this rate. You're just going to have to give up some of your outside interests."

"Yes, Joe," she said in mocking agreement. "Good-bye, Joe."

"Good-bye."

She smiled and shook her head, and called Caroline to say they would come. She was surprised to hear a note of hesitancy in Caroline's voice, and she was a bit of annoyed as well, for she and Joe could certainly think of many more pleasurable ways to spend that time than out with Caroline and Tim Somers. But Caroline had been disturbed by something lately, Jennifer reminded herself, and going out as a foursome was the cousinly and unselfish thing to do.

Jennifer didn't see Joe for the rest of the week. Jerry Loomis, manager of the new Fort Worth plant, hadn't come in to New York after all, and Joe had instead gone to see him there.

By Saturday Jennifer was wildly anxious to see

Joe. She had thought of their lovemaking over and over, recalled their "official first day," thought of his smile and laugh and handsome blue eyes. And she couldn't wait either to tell him her idea for the Ardence promotional campaign. As she sat in front of the mirror brushing her hair, however, all she wished was that she could banish a persistent and unwelcome thought. *All this happiness can't last; it's too good to be true.*

But when Joe arrived her worries disappeared. His eyes were filled with love, his arms strong with warmth as he gathered her up and held her against him wordlessly, her head against his shoulder. "God, how I missed you," he murmured. "Two lousy days, and I missed you." He drew his head back and looked into her eyes. "You know, that isn't at all the type of thing I usually have in mind—missing someone like that."

She gazed into deep blue. "It's the price you have to pay," she murmured.

"And, Lord, is it worth it," he said huskily, grazing his lips over hers. His tongue parted them and sought the warm sweetness of her mouth, and when her tongue met the tip of his, a tremor of desire coursed through her, making her tremble and hold him close.

He drew his head back. "Now I suppose you're going to tell me we're due to meet Caroline and Tim at eight or something silly like that."

She smiled. "I suppose I am," she said hazily, "since we are."

"And I suppose you wouldn't want to be late," he breathed, lips brushing hers. The touch was incredibly soft, sending pleasure to every part of her body, every part of her soul.

"I . . . could be convinced," she said, smiling. "Perhaps."

He took a long, deep breath. "Just how late would you consider being?" he murmured, holding her against his hard frame.

The movement and pressure of his chest against her breasts made her nipples harden, and she answered his question with her lips, sliding them along his neck to the tip of his ear, to his warm wet lips and enticing tongue.

He groaned and ran a hand along the small of her back, holding her so she could feel his hard thighs and the strength of his desire. He edged her lower lip between his teeth, covered her lips with his again, then trailed a heated path of damp kisses along her neck. When he reached the soft skin of her breasts, she buried her face in his hair and held him close. With a muffled moan he raised her blouse, his breath hot against her skin, and his lips closed over her breast, edging it to a taut peak of fiery desire.

"Joe," she moaned, running her hands along his strong shoulders, his firmly muscled back.

His teeth gently raked her nipple, and then his lips closed over it, and Jennifer was engulfed in shimmering, liquid waves of need. "Joe," she murmured, her voice ragged with desire.

He raised his head, his eyes hooded and cloudy with passion, his breath quick and urgent.

As if of one body, one soul, they began to walk to the bedroom.

And then the phone rang, sounding as loud and jarring as an alarm.

"Don't answer it," Joe said huskily, and with his arm firm around her waist, led her along toward the bedroom.

"I have to," she said.

He turned his head to look at her.

"I just have to," she said simply. "It's—"

He shook his head. "Then go ahead."

As she broke away from him and headed for the phone in the bedroom, she silently cursed herself for being such a slave to habit. But it was a habit she simply couldn't break.

But when she answered, it was only Caroline.

"Jennifer. God! I'm glad I caught you. Listen. We're going to be about an hour late."

"What?"

"We . . . well, Tim's hung up somewhere. I don't know. Anyway, I didn't want you to get to my place when I wasn't there. I'm at Tim's and he's coming in a while."

Jennifer sighed with annoyance. "Look, Caroline. Why don't we just forget the whole thing, all right? First it's one thing and then it's another, and I just can't—"

"What? *One* change, Jennifer. An hour later, that's all."

Jennifer looked at Joe standing in the doorway of the bedroom, leaning casually against the door frame. Of course the mood had been broken. But it could easily be recaptured. . . .

"I don't know, Caroline. Is it really that important to you?"

"Yes," Caroline moaned. "Really. Please."

She sounded desperate. Jennifer looked apologetically at Joe as she said, "All right. We'll be there." Joe rolled his eyes, but he was smiling.

When Jennifer hung up and began walking toward Joe, he held up his palms. "Uh-uh. Keep your distance, Jennifer. I'm not going through that twice in one night." He laughed. "Ten minutes after we got started, Caroline would call again."

"But, Joe. We don't have to meet them for an hour, and Caroline's apartment is only—"

"An hour, Jen, is not what I have in mind," he cut in, coming forward. When he reached her, he put an arm around her and bent slightly, gently passing his lips across hers. "I want to spend the night with you, Jennifer, and take every minute of all those hours to show you why."

She closed her eyes and leaned her head back as his lips melted into hers, and she put her arms around him and urged him forward.

He tore his mouth away. "Later," he said huskily. "And I don't plan to be sorry we waited," he added and, taking her by the hand, led her out to the foyer. "Now, since we're not due at Caroline's for an hour, why don't we go out and walk on the promenade by the river? It's a beautiful night and I'd like to talk to you about something, anyway, without any interruptions."

"Sounds fine to me." She picked up her purse and began walking toward Joe and the door, but Joe's expression—of disbelief, it looked like—stopped her. "What's wrong?" she asked.

131

"What you're wearing," he said. "Aren't you going to cover yourself with something?"

She smiled. "Are you kidding? We're not going to church, Joe, just to a restaurant for dinner."

"So that everyone can see what I see as I'm looking at you now?"

Jennifer shrugged. "I don't see why not. People see much more on any beach in America, and more on most European beaches."

"I'm not talking about European beaches, American beaches, or anything but here and now, Jennifer. Your dress is a little . . ." He hesitated.

She smiled. "Low cut?" she finished for him.

He only scowled in answer. The neckline of her dress had never struck her as particularly revealing, certainly not for evening wear. None of her other dates had ever complained about it. She thought about mentioning that to Joe, but then restrained herself. It would probably only make him madder.

Jennifer laughed; she hadn't realized he was so old-fashioned in some ways. So possessive. "I'll bring a sweater, Joe, but I'm not going to wear it unless I'm cold. I'm afraid you'll just have to share me—in some ways—with others."

He glared, but she could see the hint of a smile as she took his arm and they left her apartment.

As they walked into Carl Schurz Park at Eighty-sixth Street, Jennifer smiled to herself. She was finally half of a couple—and a couple in the park, no less. For years, especially on Sunday mornings and early-summer evenings like tonight, she had seen happy-looking couples strolling along, and they had always

132

made her feel alone and sad, forced to look at an aspect of her life she was trying to ignore.

They walked through the park toward the river, and then south along the river's edge, with the skylines of Long Island City and Roosevelt Island stark and clear against the dusky horizon.

"We're . . . in rather hot water," Joe said slowly, holding her arm a bit more tightly. He looked down at her, his eyes filled with sadness. "More than you can imagine, Jen. I hope I didn't steer you wrong in coming to Eton." He sighed. "But I think it was a mistake."

Jennifer ignored the chill that had just shot through her veins and quietly asked why.

Joe took a deep breath before he spoke. "I hope I'm wrong. But the reason I went out to see Jerry Loomis in Fort Worth rather than his coming to see me is that they're having big problems out there, with the unions, among other things. The contract is coming up for renegotiation, and we're simply not going to be able to give them a decent increase with our bottom line as rotten as it is."

Jennifer frowned. "Are you and the union basically in agreement though? Theoretically, I mean?"

Joe shrugged. "As much as we possibly can be. I think their demands are basically reasonable. My God, with inflation what it is, I don't know how any of the guys with families manage to survive." He shook his head. "The problem isn't with me, and unfortunately the solution isn't either. The board can overrule me, oust me, anything they want on this issue. And what it all comes down to is that our sales projections for the spring are as low as they've been

133

in years." He turned and looked at Jennifer. "What this all means in terms of you and me, Jen, I don't know. It could mean the end for both of us at Eton if they oust me and a new president wants to bring in his own people. It might mean nothing at all. I just want you to be prepared though."

Jennifer sighed. "It's difficult working under a guillotine, Joe. I just can't look for another job right now. With Civette, and now this, it would look as if I were a jinx. You're smiling, but that's how people really think and feel underneath all the numbers talk. 'Look at her past, Al. Every company she works for bites the dust' is what they'd say."

"We're not biting the dust, Jennifer. I don't even know what the odds are. As I said, I just wanted to warn you. And also let you know how important it is that we all work our butts off. I want to hear about anything you can come up with, any ideas, no matter how way out. If you *dream* something, I want to hear about it."

Jennifer smiled. "I don't think my dreams would go over too well with the board, especially my dreams about you. But I did think through the idea I mentioned for Ardence."

"Shoot then. I'll take practically anything at this point."

Jennifer would have appreciated a bit more enthusiasm and confidence on his part, but she knew, too, that those were difficult qualities to muster when your livelihood and career were in jeopardy. "Well. Remember the concept you started out with for Ardence? The woman with the pirate?"

Joe smiled. "The ridiculous fantasy."

"Well, how about the *un*-ridiculous fantasy? We'll have a contest. Send us your fantasy of what you'd like to have happen when you wear Ardence. Quote the label, 'Live in the heat of the moment,' and send us a story, true or imagined, a hundred words or less. And the prize will be a trip for two—you and the one you love—anywhere in the world."

Joe stopped walking and put his hands on Jennifer's shoulders. "I love it," he said enthusiastically. "I love it and I think the board will love it too." He smiled. "And I like the spirit."

She smiled. "Well, at first I was going to have it be, write us a fantasy about wearing Ardence that came true. But it was manipulative, and also silly. Who could or would check? I think this one can be fun. And we'll have a point-of-sale display in every one of our better outlets, drug and department stores, the usual."

His eyes shined into hers. "Damn it, I love it. And we're going to save the damned company with it if it's the last thing we do. But, Jennifer, have you told anyone about this yet?"

"No, just you."

"Well, don't until we make it official. I want this completely under wraps.

She shrugged. "Fine. And you don't have to make a point of it, Joe. We *are* on the same side. And it *was* my idea."

"And you *are* still sensitive about that when there's no need to be," he said, mimicking her speech rhythm.

"Then you needn't have mentioned it," she breathed. Which was true, she felt. He would never have said anything about keeping an idea secret to anyone else at her corporate level. Confidentiality was understood virtually all the time.

The conversation shifted to other topics as Jennifer and Joe walked along the river in the fading evening light. But when they left the park at Eighty-fourth Street to go to Caroline's, Joe looked into Jennifer's eyes and said, "I'm sorry about what I said, Jen."

"It's okay," she answered. And, gazing into his eyes, she wondered how she could stay angry at him for anything.

At Caroline's apartment, on the nineteenth floor of a modern luxury high-rise, the atmosphere was tense from the moment Joe and Jennifer arrived. When Jennifer, shocked by the opulence of the apartment, complimented Caroline, Caroline was evasive, murmuring that the apartment had come furnished, and quickly changed the subject. And when Tim arrived a few minutes later Caroline was submissive almost to the point of seeming frightened. It was a side of Caroline that Jennifer had never before glimpsed, and she didn't altogether like it.

Joe was tense as well, greeting Tim coolly and doing nothing to hide the fact that he hadn't wanted to come in the first place.

Jennifer, feeling as if she were the only adult present, tried to guide the conversation as they left the apartment and headed for the restaurant, but it wasn't easy. Tim and Joe responded monosyllabically to virtually all comments and questions, and Caroline kept deferring to Tim, even when Jennifer, in a

pathetic last-ditch effort, started t...
weather.

But once they were seated at the res...
pretty seafood place on the corner of...
Street and Second Avenue, Tim cam...
some standards he came a bit too stro...
talking loudly and ordering the waiter to...
snapping his fingers. But Jennifer preferre...
earlier near silence.

After they had all ordered and the drinks...
brought to the table, Tim raised his martini a...
"A toast, okay?"

Everyone else raised a glass.

"To lots more nights like tonight," he said. "...
line and I want to get out more, see more people,...
know?" He smiled, his small, pearly teeth white i...
pale face. "We've got to take advantage of this c...
more and spend less time indoors, if you know wha...
I mean. So a toast, everyone, to more of the same."

Jennifer smiled politely and drank, but she could
hardly believe what Tim was saying. He seemed utterly sincere, which meant he had to be utterly blind.
So far the evening had been painfully awkward.

"So tell me, Jenny—"

"Jennifer," she corrected.

"Jennifer then. Pretty name. Tell me, how's the
new job?"

"Oh, it's great," she said, glad for a new topic of
conversation. "It's exciting working for a small company. You know, Civette was enormous by the time
I finally left."

"Yeah," Tim said absently. "But Eton's not in
such great shape." He looked at Joe. "No offense,

but it's in all the papers. Doesn't that make it a
rough? Working under the old ax?"

"We're hardly working under an ax," Jennifer
. "As a matter of fact, we have plans—"

"—that cannot be revealed at this time," Joe cut
"But we have plans that should prove rather
ofitable," he finished.

Jennifer's fingers were white against her glass as
he clenched it, trying to stay calm. The way Joe had
ut her off had been completely humiliating, and had
mplied a serious lack of trust on his part. Why had
he assumed she was going to reveal some privileged
information?

Her only consolation was that neither Tim nor
Caroline had seemed to notice, but it was small comfort.

Tim had merely winked and said, "Gotcha. I understand," and finished his drink.

Now there was an awkward silence, and Jennifer
decided to let someone else end it. She was through
helping things along tonight in this group.

"So," Tim said, steepling his fingers. "Joe, it was
real nice of you to give our Caroline a job." He
winked. "She isn't always the easiest little girl to
handle."

"I'm not a little girl," Caroline put in, though her
tone of voice had indeed been childlike.

"She's going to improve too, I promise that." Tim
chuckled. "Otherwise she's just going to have to
work for me, and that's something I stay away from
—mixing business and pleasure."

"Then let us," Joe said coldly, "if you don't mind,
discuss something other than business."

The smile that had been plastered on Tim's face disappeared, and there was another silence.

But Jennifer hardly noticed. She couldn't stop thinking about Joe's lack of trust.

Finally, what seemed like ages later, Jennifer and Joe said good night to Caroline and Tim and headed back to Jennifer's apartment.

The silence that lay between them was unpleasant, lingering because each was deep in thought. Jennifer marveled at how she had felt earlier when she had thought she could never stay angry at Joe for anything. And now she was smarting from a few words he had said hours earlier.

"I'm still angry," she said quietly, walking along beside him. He hadn't taken her arm.

"So am I," he said.

"You!" She turned to face him. "What do *you* have to be upset about?"

"How about a rotten evening I never wanted to undergo in the first place, compounded by a totally silent date? You didn't open your mouth to help the conversation along one bit."

She smiled coldly. "As I recall, it was quite the contrary until I was so rudely cut off."

"I cut you off because I didn't know what you were going to say," he said.

"That's right," she snapped. "You didn't know what I was going to say. So you shouldn't have assumed."

They arrived at her building, and Jennifer was tempted to tell him to go home. When she met his eyes he said, "I'd like to come up, all right? At the very least we should talk this through."

She muttered a cold "All right," and they rode up in the elevator in tense silence. As Jennifer walked quickly down the hallway and opened the door to her apartment, she was aware of Joe right behind her as of a hostile presence.

When they were in the foyer she turned to him. "You're always talking about talking things through, Joe. Working things out. I think it's time you worked out the small matter of trust between us. I know it was a small thing, your cutting me off, but it felt awful, as if I were a child."

"No one noticed," he said.

"Those two wouldn't have noticed if we had set the table on fire, Joe. *I* noticed."

"I'm sorry," he said, gazing into her eyes. She looked away, telling herself she was being manipulated. He knew his blue eyes could cut through so much. "I'm sorry," he repeated, "but I couldn't take the chance. At that moment, Jen, it was more important that a company confidence remain a confidence than that I not hurt you. I don't trust Somers one bit." He sighed and ran a hand through his hair. "As a matter of fact, I wish Caroline weren't seeing him."

Jennifer stared at him unbelievingly. "You wish? Well, then why don't you just command her to stop? My God, Joe, do you hear yourself? Your employees aren't your slaves. They can see whomever they want."

"Fine," he shot back. "But I don't have to participate in their social lives." He stepped forward and put his hands on her waist. For a moment her eyes closed as she tried to fight the tide of warmth flowing from his touch. "Jennifer, it's *you* I want to see. Not you and a cast of thousands." His fingers moved under her blouse, and his touch was hot and firm against her skin as he traced the curve of her waist. "I've thought of you for days. And I don't want to share the time we have with anyone else." His thumbs edged along her rib cage, moving upward across smooth skin. "You have to understand," he said huskily, leaning forward and trailing his lips along her neck. "Understand that I might be blunt or brusque or even rude when I'm annoyed that someone's keeping us apart." His lips brushed across hers and he pulled back, enveloping her in his gaze. "That someone sometimes includes you when you put obstacles in the path of our being together. To keep it safe, to keep it controlled." He took a long, deep breath. "I don't want it controlled, Jennifer. I don't want it safe." His hands suddenly moved upward and covered her breasts, making her weak with desire. He brushed each nipple with his fingertips, charging her with a tantalizing need that spiraled through her body. He trailed his lips along her ear. "And I don't give a damn about anything or anyone but you right now. Making love to you is all that matters," he said hoarsely. "At this moment Caroline could be going out with my worst enemy and I wouldn't care. Tell the world our secrets and I wouldn't care."

"But what about later on?" she murmured, inhaling his familiar scent as she buried her lips in his neck. "I have to know. . . ." Her voice trailed off. What she had to know, she realized, what all her

141

other questions were merely substitutes for, was whether or not he loved her. Her uncertainty was the source of all her questions, all her doubts. But she'd sooner live in uncertainty than ask and hear an answer she didn't want to hear.

"Talk to me," he murmured. "Tell me. Ask me what you want to know." He gazed into her eyes. "All I want to do is please you, Jen. Every way I know how."

But words and questions left as she was enveloped in his heated grasp, and she moaned with a cry of need born of their first time together, when she had learned the shimmering heights of ecstasy his touch could bring. She wanted him again so much she ached. "Oh, Joe," she murmured, running her lips along his neck. "It's so difficult to fight you."

"Then don't," he whispered. "Come with me instead," he urged. And he lifted her into his arms and carried her off to the bedroom.

When he placed her gently on the bed, she sat up to undress, but he shook his head. "Please," he said softly. "It's so damn exciting for me to do."

"I'm glad," she whispered.

He slipped her silk top over her head, and when she lowered her arms, he moaned and cupped her breasts in his hands. His touch ignited her as it never had. She knew what he could give her, knew their perfect rhythm, and she wanted it now. "I need you," she said breathlessly, reaching for him.

"Oh, Jennifer," he whispered. And in seconds, he had taken off the rest of her clothes and his own.

Lying together, they explored each other languorously yet urgently, bringing each other to the brink

142

over and over again in liquefying smoldering touches, long, deep kisses, and arching thrusts. Jennifer cried out for him as she felt the strength of his desire tremble under her touch, heard him moan her name with an urgency that aroused her to a melting heat.

"I want you *now*," she cried, arching beneath him, raking his back.

And once again they were united in a blaze of passion that released everything but pleasure and sensation from Jennifer's mind.

Afterward, as they lay in each other's arms, Jennifer held Joe close as he nuzzled her forehead with his warm lips. "That was so wonderful," he murmured. "So beautiful." He stroked her hair. "And we're all right, right?" He shifted so he could look into her eyes. "You're not still angry at me then?"

She smiled and lazily shook her head. "No, I'm not still angry at you," she murmured, barely remembering what he was referring to.

"I'm just sorry I have to leave soon," he whispered. He hugged her tightly against him. "But I'll be back."

She smiled. "I know," she whispered. "I know."

NINE

The next morning Jennifer woke up feeling wonderful. When she turned over onto her stomach and inhaled the lingering essence of Joe's scent, she was filled with the memory of their lovemaking, filled with a carefree sense of things she had never had before. Feeling as deliciously blissful as she had last night was possible, and would be possible again, only if she didn't constantly worry about what Joe's exact feelings for her were. The message was clear that he cared deeply for her. How else could the lovemaking have been so tender and passionate, so gentle and yet so deep?

A bit later, on her way to work, she realized with a smile that after all her worrying over what people at Eton might think of the affair, nothing at all had happened. People had thought she was sleeping with Joe long before she had in fact been doing so, and their interest, for the most part, had turned to other things—primarily whether rumored layoffs were going to take place. But Jennifer was optimistic about Eton's future as well, for she knew that two important developments could help the company tremendously: the new Ardence campaign, and the new product line, Amino-Actives. So far both were still in the planning stages, but it looked as if the board were going to approve both at their next meeting.

When Jennifer arrived at work she decided to drop in on Joe to avoid another awkward morning-after. *This* morning she knew he wasn't interested only in business, and it would be nice to see him and kiss him hello. She knew he had no morning appointments.

But when she began sailing past his secretary, Laura, and called out, "He's in, isn't he?" she was caught up short by the young woman's plaintive "Wait!"

Jennifer stopped and turned around, and Laura widened her eyes apologetically. "I'm sorry, Miss Preston. I didn't mean to yell. Only Mr. Brennan specifically said he wants no calls and no visitors."

Jennifer frowned. "What's up? Do you know?"

Laura shrugged. "All I know is that he's in the worst mood I've ever seen him in. Maybe he had a bad night or something." She paled then and quickly said, "I mean, I don't know. I guess . . . it's personal. I mean it's none of my business."

Jennifer nodded absently. What had happened between last night and this morning to so upset Joe? And if nothing had happened, did that mean he was in a bad mood *because* of last night? Jennifer took a deep breath. "Laura, buzz him and tell him I'd like to see him."

"I don't know, Miss Preston. He specifically said, 'I don't want to hear that goddamn buzzer.'"

"Never mind. If no one else is in there, I'll just go in myself."

Without giving herself a chance to back out—after all, she was Joe's lover, his "official and only girl friend," as he had put it—she knocked on the door, called in, "Joe, it's Jennifer," and opened the door.

He looked up from his desk, as startled and angry as she had ever seen him. His eyes were pale and cold, frightening in their distance.

"Is everything all right?" Jennifer asked, shutting the door behind her. "Laura said you were upset about something."

He sighed. "Laura should know better."

"I'm not just one of a crowd, Joe. I'm sure she knew she—"

"Whatever she knows or doesn't know, she damn well doesn't have the right—" He reached for the phone.

"Stop," Jennifer cut in. "I came in here myself because she didn't want to disturb you. All right? Now tell me what's going on." She tried to reach him with her eyes, to communicate without words, as they did so well together. But she reached only coldness.

"Sit down," he said quietly, his voice laced with reluctance. His tone was bone-chilling in its formality, and as Jennifer sat down she was weak with apprehension. Was he about to tell her it was all over, that the relationship wasn't working out? That last night had been the final one? She wished she hadn't braved her way past Laura. She had been so happy and carefree all morning that she hadn't even realized that barging in on Joe at what was a difficult time was an act of blind insensitivity. But it was too late.

He sighed, picked up a newspaper, and tossed it to Jennifer's edge of the desk. "Read that," he said. "Second column."

It was *Cosmetics News,* dated that morning. At the top of the second column, Jennifer began reading:

> Ailing Eton Cosmetics, in an attempt to bolster its reddening bottom line, is planning a new product line for a targeted 25–40 female age group. Aimed at "the woman who knows what she wants," the line will be called Amino-Actives, reflecting the high-protein content of all products in the line. Though plans have not been finalized, company sources reveal that Eton intends to promote the line heavily as a "good-for-you" beauty regimen, with TV and radio spots bolstering print ads and promotion.

Jennifer put the paper down and looked at Joe. "Our whole campaign," she said quietly.

He looked annoyed. "More important than that, Jennifer. It endangers the trademark."

"Have you spoken to *Cosmetics News*?" she asked.

He shook his head. "I want to avoid that if I possibly can. When I called them about the first item, they couldn't have been less pleasant or cooperative. The paper has been acquired by some new people, you know. Anyway, I don't want the publicity to get any more negative than it already is."

"But you could sue," she said.

He slammed the desk with his hand. "Goddamn it, Jennifer, this company is in trouble. I am *not* going to sink thousands of dollars into a lawsuit right now." He shook his head. "I just don't know what the hell's going on here anymore. One or two articles —that could happen to anyone. But what happened today was really damaging. And there's no question about it—the information came from inside."

Jennifer rolled the edge of the paper between her fingers. "Do you have any idea who it might be?" she asked quietly. The scene was so reminiscent of six years earlier—the leak, the suspicion, the uncertainty—that she could hardly find her voice.

"None," he snapped. "It could be anyone."

She gazed at him levelly. His tone had been sharp, unkind even. "Not *any*one," she said.

"Jennifer, I have to work this out alone," he said tiredly.

She stared, her throat constricting around tears of anger and hurt. "Fine," she said hollowly, and stood up. "Let me know when you've worked it out," she said, and turned and walked to the door.

"Jennifer!"

She opened the door, walked out, and shut the door quietly behind her.

With the painful scene echoing in her mind, she went down the hall to her office, but once in decided to leave. Absently saying good-bye to Sherry, she left the office with a pile of work and headed back for her apartment.

She could hardly believe it, but Joe's manner and words had been clear. He trusted no one. Including her. Images of their lovemaking, of their laughter, of their shared embraces and dreams, flashed through her mind and brought tears to her eyes. Could this man with whom she had shared so much trust her so little? The iciness of his replies had been more painful even than his words. It would have been better had he said, "Jennifer, did you do it?" than that reptilian evasiveness.

Jennifer, once home, did an enormous amount of work that afternoon. It was the only way she was able to stop thinking about Joe, the only way she could shut her mind off from everything except the market analysis she was doing. Later, when she took a break to go grocery shopping, she walked through the store mechanically, came home, and immediately went back to work.

When she finished she looked at her watch and saw that it was only four o'clock, and with a wave of melancholy realized she couldn't avoid thinking about Joe forever. No, at some point she would have to face the truth, the truth that said Joe had not been what she had imagined, and the relationship had not been what she had imagined.

The doorbell rang, and Jennifer absently got up from the couch, grateful that the groceries had arrived and she could distract herself by making dinner.

But when she opened the door, it was Joe standing there. A startled "Oh!" was all she managed to say.

He tilted his head. "May I come in?"

"Are you sure you want to?" she asked coldly.

"Fraternizing with industrial spies doesn't look too good for a company president."

His lips tightened and he stepped past her. "Come on, Jennifer."

She let the door slam shut and whirled to face him. "No, *you* come on, Joe. You may not like the words, but you as much as accused me of being involved in that leak today. And to patronize me by saying, 'oh, come on,' as if it's in my imagination, or forgotten, is an insult."

For a moment Jennifer thought she saw a flash of pain in Joe's eyes. But it disappeared as he said, "It *is* in your imagination, Jen, or let's say it was a misunderstanding, and—"

"A misunderstanding!" she cried. "Who do you think you are, that you can stand there and calmly tell me it was a misunderstanding? Don't you know how it felt, having you suspect—"

"But I didn't," he cut in. "Damn it, Jennifer, I'm not a mindreader and I'm also not perfect. That leak was exactly what I didn't need to have happen, and I reacted." He sighed. "And one reason I had wanted to be alone was that I didn't want to get angry and hurt someone I didn't want to hurt, or act in a way I'd regret later on." He paused. "I wanted to be alone, Jen, and if that meant driving you away, I suppose that unconsciously that was more appealing than having you see me like that."

She shook her head. "You can't censor your feelings like that, Joe. I do the same thing, and it leads to no good. I guess . . . I guess part of me knew you couldn't really suspect me, but you were so . . . you were so cold."

Joe stepped forward and put his hands over her arms. "I'm sorry," he said quietly. "I had to do a lot of thinking. And I was really angry. But I'm not going to do what I did six years ago. I'm not going to go on a wild goose chase to find out who's responsible, not if it means hurting someone who's innocent. I want you to know that."

She nodded. "I'm glad."

"But, Jen, what bothers me most about what happened today is the lack of trust between us." He frowned. "If you really thought that of me"—he bent down and kissed her lightly on the lips—"how can you really trust me?" He ran his hands down to her waist and held her tightly, looking into her eyes with a deep blue that made her forget all that had just happened. "And if you don't really trust me," he said huskily, pulling her close against his firm frame, "how can you reach the heights of pleasure, give yourself to me more fully each and every time?"

"Oh, Joe." She shook her head. "I do trust you"— she paused—"when I'm in your arms," she murmured, caressing his chest, "or when we're making love."

He inhaled sharply. "Then let me hold you," he said huskily. "and love you, and show you that I trust you so that you'll never forget."

She smiled.

Moments later they were lying naked in bed. Joe leaned over her face and gazed at her with heavy-lidded eyes cloudy with passion. And then he trailed his lips from her neck downward, stopping to kiss and nuzzle the rise of each breast, each nipple, in an incredibly arousing kiss.

"Joe," she murmured, running her fingers through his hair.

"Give yourself to me completely, Jen," he whispered, his mouth descending as she cried out in pleasure. "Let's not doubt each other ever again."

"Oh, yes," she moaned, whispering his name.

And they were together then, ascending the peaks of ecstasy they had come to know so well, crying out each other's names in rolling, coursing passion that plunged them into an explosion of pleasure.

Slowly they edged over into the depths of satisfaction and completeness, breathless and damp, holding each other close.

And after kissing each other and smiling into each other's eyes, limbs entwined, they languorously fell asleep.

The next morning Joe woke Jennifer up with a kiss on each eyelid and whispered he was leaving.

She opened her mouth to protest, but he covered her lips in a long deep kiss and then drew back, smiling. "I'd never leave," he murmured, "if I had my way. Just promise me one thing, Jen."

She smiled lazily. "Anything."

"I'll act like a reasonably sane human being at the office if you will." He smiled. "If I see you, I won't act as if I hardly know you, and you'll do the same. If I say something you don't like, you'll tell me, and I'll do the same. All right?"

"Sounds fine to me. Just one thing though."

He raised a brow. "Yes?"

"At the meeting today . . ."

"Yes?"

"If you look at me with those bedroom eyes, I'm going to have to pretend it's not happening. Otherwise—"

"Oh, Jen," he murmured, and pulled her into his arms.

When Jennifer got to her office—an hour late—she found Caroline sitting in her chair at the desk. Caroline jumped up. "Oh! Jennifer. I didn't hear you come in." Nervously, as if unaware of her movements, Caroline sat and then stood again, watching like a child as Jennifer hung up her trench coat.

"Sorry. Here," Caroline said, standing and gesturing for the chair. She moved and sat in front of the desk as Jennifer took her seat.

"How are you?" Jennifer asked. "I haven't seen you in a while."

Caroline stared at the desk. At first Jennifer thought Caroline hadn't heard her. But then her cousin began slowly shaking her head from side to side. And when she finally looked up at Jennifer, tears welled up in her eyes and streamed down her cheeks.

"Hon, what *is* it?" Jennifer cried, reaching out a hand to Caroline's.

Caroline shook her head more quickly. "Don't. You should hate me. I shouldn't even be here. Maybe in jail, but not here. God. I hate myself."

"Caroline, what is it?"

Caroline wiped the tears from her eyes, looked at Jennifer, and burst out crying again. "Well, for one thing," she wailed, sniffling and dabbing at her eyes, "Tim and I broke up. It's totally over."

"I'm sor—"

"Don't be. I hate him. I mean I don't, but I do. Oh, I don't know what I mean." She glanced at Jennifer and then looked away. "But the worst part is what I've done." She looked directly into Jennifer's eyes. "I'm the one who was responsible for those articles in *Cosmetics News.*"

"What?"

Caroline breathed quickly and went on, speaking rapidly and in a high voice. "It didn't seem like a big thing at first. I mean, at first I didn't even know I was giving Tim information." She forced a laugh. "I just thought he was real interested in my work. And in me, obviously. I mean, he just asked a lot of questions. But then he needed more"—she shrugged— "and he made it seem as if I wasn't doing anything wrong, Jennifer."

She paused, on the verge of tears, and then continued in a tiny voice. "I kind of loved him, I guess. And he got me my apartment and stuff, and paid for it, and it seemed as if . . . I thought he loved me." She sighed. "And he kind of advised me on things— what to do at work, stuff like that. It felt great having someone look after me and care about me." She smiled sadly, and the smile twisted into a frown. "When I didn't like Joe Brennan at first, Tim told me I was right, and that he was really an awful guy. And, Jennifer, I had thought you were still against Joe Brennan."

"But I was *working* for him, Caroline. And then, well, Joe and I *are* kind of involved."

Caroline looked away. "I know. That's what I feel the worst about," she said quietly. "I just couldn't stop. I saw no reason to stop, 'cause Tim told me what I was doing was real minor, and people do it every day at every company in the world." She sighed. "But when I finally really wanted to pull out, he frightened me. He said that you and Joe would find out it was me. He'd make sure you found out. And he wanted us all to go out together. He actually wanted to become *friendly* with Joe, can you imagine, so he could get little bits and pieces of information here and there. He'd do anything." She paused, her lower lip starting to tremble. "And I think it's probably true," she said slowly, her voice thin and strained, "that the only reason he went out with me was because of the whole business." Her face twisted into a sob, and she began crying again.

Jennifer rose and went around the desk to comfort Caroline. "I'm sure that's not true, honey," she said quietly. "And if it was, he wasn't worth it. You know that. And it's all over now."

Caroline shook her head. "What about *me* though? You've got to promise not to tell," she cried. "And I promise I'll change." She looked hopefully at Jennifer. "I *have* changed. You know, when I was in California I did a lot of shoplifting, and stuff like that, and when I got here, I kind of kept it up a little. Like that dress I wore to that charity thing, remember?"

Jennifer nodded. So that was why Caroline had been so evasive.

"Well, that was the last dress I lifted, Jen. Forever." She widened her eyes. "So will you not tell, Jen?"

Jennifer sighed. A few moments earlier she

wouldn't have even hesitated about remaining silent. Caroline was her cousin and needed help. But now she was beginning to feel manipulated in the face of Caroline's puppy-brown eyes and promises of sincere reform. Jennifer was neither her mother nor her chaperon: she didn't need testaments of change.

"Jennifer, please? Mr. Brennan wouldn't understand. He doesn't really know me. And if I'm going to stop, what's the harm?"

"The harm, Caroline, is that now I either lie to Joe or hurt you in a way I'd rather not. That's the harm," she said harshly.

"But if you tell, I'll lose my job. And then where will I be? How can that help, Jennifer?" She paused, and added in a small voice, "Please?"

Jennifer looked into Caroline's eyes. "You promise it's all over," she said firmly, "and I'll promise I'll do my best to help you and to keep it to myself. All right?"

Caroline nodded quickly. "I promise. I promise."

"Okay. Now tell me all about it from the beginning. I want to know everything you did."

TEN

After Caroline left, Jennifer buzzed Sherry and asked her to hold all calls. She had a pounding headache, and as she began rummaging in her purse for aspirin she realized she had the kind of headache that probably wouldn't go away until she unraveled her feelings about Caroline and what she had done. As she thought of Joe's agonizing over the articles from *Cosmetics News* —his face haggard and drawn with fatigue—her head pounded more, the muscles constricting as if in a vise.

She finally found her bottle of aspirin, and left the office to get some water.

Halfway down the corridor, she saw Joe stepping out of someone's office. He didn't see her—his back had been turned, and now he was walking in the same direction as Jennifer—but Jennifer stopped in her tracks, the pain pounding more than ever.

She didn't want to see him, not now, not if she had

to lie to him, and when she began walking again, she walked slowly, hanging back so she wouldn't catch up with him.

But somehow, through a sixth sense or chance, Joe glanced back just as he got to his office.

He drew his head back as if surprised, and smiled. "Well," he said, looking at her appreciatively as she came up to him, "you certainly got yourself in here quickly enough. Come on in, Jen. I want to talk to you about something."

Jennifer hesitated. "Actually, Joe, I've got a terrible headache. Can it wait?"

He smiled. "Sure. It was just a kiss." He tilted his head and gazed at her with pleasure. "But I suppose it can wait until tonight."

Tonight, Jennifer thought. Would she be able to be with him, knowing she was holding back, keeping something from him that he very much wanted to know? "Uh, Joe."

"Hmm?"

"About tonight. Let's skip it, okay?" He frowned, but she went on. "Let's make it sometime later in the week."

He studied her, penetrating her eyes, looking for a clue she simply wouldn't give. "All right," he said. "If that's the way you want it. May I ask why?"

She felt awful. Now she would compound the lie, add to something she didn't want to have exist in the first place. "It's nothing, really," she said vaguely. "I mean nothing specific."

He raised a brow. "I've heard those words before, Jen. Coming from me. I think I understand," he said quietly. His gaze melted into hers for a few brief seconds, then grew cold and distant. "By the way, when you get back to your office, Sherry will tell you there's a meeting of the department heads this afternoon—two o'clock. See you then," he said hollowly, and turned and went into the office, shutting the door quietly behind him.

Jennifer closed her eyes and leaned against the wall, fighting the well of sadness rising inside. The look of pain and then distance she had seen in Joe's eyes was something she would never forget. And the sadness in his voice, edged with huskiness that came from a passion the other side of desire. She had hurt him and hurt herself badly.

She sighed. If he were different—aggressively questioning like Andrew Cole, say—he would have cross-examined her until she had said something, anything, that he considered a "good reason" for their being apart. But Joe was delicate in his own way, too sensitive to pry, feeling—as she, too, always did—that it was better to be uncertain than to hear unwanted words.

Later on in the afternoon, as Jennifer left her office for the department-heads meeting, her head still hurt, though the pain seemed less real than the pain of thinking about Joe. She would have to tell him about Caroline someday—to keep something like that from him was unthinkable—but revealing the story to him now was nearly as unpleasant a thought. She had promised her cousin, and the promise had been completely sincere and heartfelt. Caroline had asked for her help, and for her silence, and to promise both and give neither would be the worst of all possible paths, dishonest at every stage of the way.

No, Caroline was counting on her, and she had made a promise she would not break.

Jennifer was the first person to enter the conference room, a large room with an oval table in the middle and gray industrial carpeting on the floor and walls. She sat down in a chair at the middle of the table, opened a folder of letters Sherry had typed, and began reading and signing them. People would probably be straggling in for the next five or ten minutes, and she didn't feel like wasting the time with boring small talk when she could be getting some work done.

Jennifer heard a footfall on the carpet and looked up. Joe had just come in and was pulling out his chair at the end of the table.

Their eyes met—so briefly as to almost have not met at all—and he nodded curtly. "Jennifer." His voice was distant, as if he were speaking to a not very well liked acquaintance.

She looked down at her work—the words meant nothing to her—and back at Joe. He was leafing through some papers, as perfunctorily as she, she suspected, and his features were rigid and ungiving.

"Joe," she said quietly.

He looked up at her, his eyes tentative.

"I'm sorry about before," she said.

"There's nothing to be sorry about," he said, "if that's the way you feel. We both know that cautiousness—perhaps overcautiousness—is a quality we share."

"But that isn't it," she said. "At least . . ." Her voice trailed off. What could she say?

"Look, Jennifer. If the goddamn rest of the group weren't such a lazy bunch of do-nothings, they'd be here already. I'd really rather discuss this some other time," he said.

She looked into his eyes, searching their meaning, but he looked away. "All right," she said. "Some other time then."

She swallowed and went back to trying to read. Joe was so unforgiving, so immovable. She had merely put off seeing him for a day or two. She hadn't said that their relationship was over. Now, it seemed, he wouldn't give her a second chance.

They sat together in silence, each pretending to read, until their colleagues began to file in. As the small talk began neither Joe nor Jennifer even bothered to look up. And by the time all eight department heads had come in and Joe began the meeting, Jennifer felt a million miles away.

"This will be short and unpleasant," Joe began.

Two people laughed, but when they saw Joe wasn't smiling, the laughter abruptly ended.

"As you all know," Joe continued, steepling his fingers, "we have a confidentiality problem here at Eton right now." He raised a brow. "Three articles in *Cosmetics News,* with no doubt more to come. The last item was certainly the most serious—possibly endangering our trademark potential for the Amino-Actives line. However, serious as the situation is, I'm not prepared to go on a witch hunt."

"Why not?" came a voice from behind Jennifer.

It was Skip DeWitt, head of the sales and service

department and one of Joe's more vocal detractors. "I think Eton's having enough trouble already without adding *this* to the heap. If we can stop it, I think we should."

Joe smiled mildly. "I couldn't agree with you more," he said calmly. "But since we don't know who's responsible, stopping him or her could prove difficult." He turned from Skip and looked at the people on the other side of the table, across from Jennifer. He had avoided her eyes since the meeting had begun.

"I think we're hiding our heads in the sand," Skip called out. "I think an investigation is in order. Why are you so against that?"

Joe raised his brows. He was known for encouraging people to speak out at meetings no matter what their level in the company. But apparently even he thought DeWitt was perhaps going too far. "My reasons, Mr. DeWitt, are rather personal." He didn't look at Jennifer, but she felt as if he did. "Suffice it to say, however, that they're moot as well. The fact of the matter is that the board wants me to proceed with an investigation." A chill ran down Jennifer's spine. "I'm meeting with someone from an agency tomorrow, and—"

"A detective agency?" someone asked.

Joe nodded. "An industrial security firm, according to their letterhead, but, yes, a detective agency. And I'd like you all—and this is more than a request, it's an order—to please, for God's sake, keep your departments calm. I'm calling a companywide meeting tomorrow. I'd like to say a few words to everyone to smooth things along a bit. But, please, say nothing today. I merely wanted to let you all know about it. And after tomorrow's meeting, do your utmost to assure everyone that . . ." He hesitated and shook his head. "Actually," he said quietly, his voice suddenly tired, "I don't know what you *can* say. It's a rotten business. Do your best. That's all I have to say."

There was a flurry of questions afterward. Joe did his best to answer them, though from his remarks and manner it was obvious that he felt it was futile to speculate about what might happen. Finally he ended the meeting rather abruptly, and people began to file out.

Jennifer lingered. She wanted to talk with Joe again, to leave things any way other than what they were. But Joe stood up and began to leave with a group of people.

"Joe!" she called.

He turned.

"Could I talk to you for a moment?"

The last group filed out, and Joe and Jennifer were alone. Joe walked slowly back in, and she came to where he stood, looking up into his eyes and seeing only the eyes of a near-stranger. "I'm sorry about what's going on," she said. "It must be very difficult for you."

"It's a very unpleasant business, yes. Especially because of the past."

They looked at each other silently.

"I'm sorry about before, Joe. And don't say there's nothing to be sorry about."

He sighed. "Jennifer, you always worried about how things would work out at the office if we became lovers. I'm sorry to say that you were right. It's very

163

difficult to talk to a group of people when I'm wondering what you're thinking, why you've said what you've said. And I'm also sorry to say that if you want a rest, a break, from what we had, I think I'd rather not see you at all than see you like this—looking at each other across a conference table, or talking in the hallway. When I see you, I want to know that the lovemaking I'm thinking about can happen that evening, that the thoughts I want to share with you won't have to wait a week."

"Then forget what I said," she answered. "Forget what I said earlier. We'll see each other tonight, as soon as you're finished here, and to hell with . . . to hell with whatever." She smiled into his eyes. "I really do want to be with you," she said softly.

His gaze merged with hers. "I'm glad," he said quietly, inhaling deeply as if taking her to him. "Come to my place? For dinner?"

"That sounds great. Eight o'clock?"

"I'll see you then," he said, and turned to leave.

"Wait a minute."

He turned around, and she took his shoulders in her grasp and covered his mouth with hers, kissing him long and hard and holding him close. She didn't care if anyone might see, she didn't care what anyone might think. All she cared about was sharing her feelings with Joe in this way that felt so natural and right.

It was the first time Jennifer had ever been to Joe's apartment, and when she arrived, she was amazed by the sparseness of it. Joe lived in a very modern building, and the blank surfaces of the walls, together with an almost total lack of furniture, created an impression of extreme starkness.

She kissed Joe hello, lingering for a moment in the pleasure of his strong arms, and then walked into the living room. There was one couch, one table and set of chairs, one painting, and one rug, in a room that would be considered large by any standards.

When she looked at Joe, he was smiling. "Like it?" he asked, a gleam in his eyes.

"Isn't it a little . . . spare?" she asked.

He laughed a deep, rich laugh. "Yes, I'd say a little spare described it rather well. Not that I want it overcrowded." He shrugged. "I've just been moving around so much over the past years. And when I wasn't moving, I was always planning to, always looking for the next place to go." He paused, looking into her eyes. "I guess I've never really known what I wanted," he said softly, "or whom." He wrapped his arms around her, pulling her close. "Until now," he murmured, his cheek against hers, his breath soft and warm against her neck.

During dinner—steak, rice, salad, and red wine— the mood was easy and relaxed. They knew they had come to an understanding, each in his own way. What was important was that they were together, no matter what. Jennifer wasn't going to think beyond that. She had learned that did no good, that one couldn't predict anyhow. Joe's feelings were strong and made up of love of a sort, if not of one she could count on. But when could one ever?

As they talked of work and dreams, the past and the future, successes and mistakes, Jennifer knew in the back of her mind that now was the best time in the world to tell Joe about Caroline. She was going to tell him someday . . . and the time was right. But she didn't want to break the mood—his smiling eyes, his deep warm laugh, his smooth, gentle voice as he recalled a memory, asked a question, told a story. No, she just couldn't say anything now . . . not yet.

But when Joe brought up the subject of the investigation, she had no choice. "The goddamn board is being such a pain in the butt about the investigation," Joe said, stirring his coffee. "And you know, there are issues over which I would consider resigning. Theoretically this is one of them. The sort of invasion of privacy they're planning is absolutely repulsive to me." He sighed. "But of all the issues I could resign over, this is the one that would be most suicidal for me. I simply couldn't do it. Resigning would look as if *I* were guilty—which wouldn't make sense, but as you said the other day, and I agree, people really don't think with their heads." He shrugged. "Anyway, I just wish there were another way, or that I had enough leverage to simply put my foot down and say, 'Hell, no.' "

Jennifer's throat was dry. She took a sip of coffee and cleared her throat. "Uh, Joe, I have to talk to you about that."

He smiled. "Our favorite topic."

"No, this is serious," she said, looking down. She took a deep breath. "Joe, I know who did it. And I know why. But before I tell you, I'd like to explain." When she looked at him, she lost much of her confidence. His eyes were aggressive and questioning.

"Go on," he said carefully.

166

"This person—the one who did it. I promised her I wouldn't tell you, and—"

"Wouldn't tell me!" he interrupted. "Jennifer, this isn't kindergarten. Now tell me what's going on."

"Don't get angry," she said, trying to sound stronger than she felt.

He merely looked at her.

"All right," she said. "In a nutshell. This person, this young woman—" She sighed. What was the point of keeping Caroline's name out if she was going to tell him in two minutes anyway? "All right. It was Caroline. My cousin."

His eyes flashed. "Caroline!" He swore softly and shook his head. "Goddamn it, Jennifer, am I going to have to fire every member of your family before I'm through with my career? Is this some sort of game with your family, let's see how fast I can get fired?"

Jennifer paled. "Say that again," she said quietly.

He looked into her eyes and shook his head. "I'm sorry," he said. "I didn't mean it. You know I didn't."

"What do you mean, you know I didn't? How am I supposed to know that, Joe?"

"Because I . . . because of the way I feel about you," he said quietly. "Because people say things they don't mean." He paused. "Now tell me what happened."

She studied his eyes. "I want to know that it's all right," she said. "I've already broken my promise of silence. At least I'd like to keep my promise to help her, Joe. And you just mentioned firing."

He shook his head. "It won't happen," he said. "Not if you don't want it to. Now tell me."

Jennifer told Joe a pared-down version of what Caroline had said. "She didn't mean to hurt you," she finished. "She thought that what she was doing was very minor. At the beginning she didn't even think she was doing anything. She thought she and Tim were just idly talking. He'd ask her about work, and she'd answer. You know Caroline."

He raised his brows. "Mmm. I can imagine."

"Anyway, Tim has a very good friend—or at least someone who owes him a favor—on *Cosmetics News.* The new owner, I think. Anyway, someone who would print just about anything he wanted as long as it was basically true. He just didn't care who the source was. And Tim fed him whatever information he could get, at the most damaging time he could. He's been doing whatever he can to make other companies look bad, and this was just one more ploy in a whole line, I imagine." She paused. "But it's all over now, Joe. Caroline doesn't want to see Tim ever again."

Joe sighed. "This puts me in a difficult position," he said, "but I'm sure I can work it out."

She looked into his eyes. "So nothing's going to happen?"

"Isn't that what you want?" He shrugged. "I know I can swing it as long as the board has my assurance that it's over"—he raised a brow—"and you're sure about that, right?"

Jennifer quickly nodded.

"Then I don't see why that won't be good enough.

And it'll save them some money too. That security firm was going to cost an arm and a leg."

Jennifer smiled. "I'm really glad, Joe, that . . . that I told you. I didn't know what to do before. And I couldn't stand lying to you. That's really why I nearly put off seeing you tonight."

He gazed into her eyes. "We have to learn to trust each other more," he said. "And we have to believe that this is true, that we're together and it's not a dream." He paused, taking in each of her features as carefully as she was taking in his. "And that we can trust each other with anything . . . and everything." His eyes bore into hers. "I've never wanted to do that with anyone before, never needed to or thought I could." He reached his hand forward and covered hers, then laced his fingers into hers. "Come with me," he said quietly, standing up.

She rose and followed him down a hall into his bedroom. In the pale moonlight coming through the window they clung to each other, looking into each other's eyes and seeing wonder and desire and love. They slowly undressed each other, prolonging the delicious wanting, the pleasure of gentle caresses as they let their clothes fall to the floor.

"You're so beautiful," he whispered. "Each time we make love," he murmured, pulling her close, "I find you more so."

As her skin touched his—warm, masculine, scented with damp desire—and she felt the strength of his thighs, the rapid beating of his heart, she moaned and brought her lips to his neck, then down to a nipple that rose enticingly to her delicate touch. She roved her mouth downward, running her hands along his chest, down along his firm stomach.

"Oh, Jennifer," he cried hoarsely, and trembled with desire. "Oh, God."

They waited no longer. There was no need, no reason. They belonged to each other, and knew that their lovemaking could be quick or slow, achingly drawn out or blazing with fiery passion. And tonight it was breathlessly fierce, explosively arousing, leaving them afterward spent and exhausted in each other's loving arms.

Jennifer awakened from a dream-delicious sleep just as the thin light of dawn was coming through Joe's window. She awakened with her senses alive and satisfied—with Joe's warm hands on her skin, his scent, the softness of his even breath against her cheek, the taste of his lips a memory she reawakened with a gentle kiss.

He awakened slowly, blissfully, his eyes opening and looking into hers with a depth of pleasure that made her heart soar.

"I'm going to go," she whispered, brushing her lips along his eyelids. "I'll see you at the office."

He pulled her on top of him and held her close, burying his face in her neck. "I treasure every moment we have," he whispered. "Every moment."

She hugged him. "So do I."

They gazed at each other, and a slow smile spread across Joe's face. "I think," he said slowly, "I think that if you're going to leave, you should leave. Or else stay for a rather invigorating good morning."

Her eyes half-closed in desire, and she smiled, but

she shook her head as well. Something had come over her—a gray cloud of melancholy—as Joe had spoken of treasuring their every moment. For she knew that their moments together could never stay this wonderful, this blissful, if they continued to be together at work as well as in love. Something would happen, something would have to come between them, as Caroline's problem almost had, and hurt the relationship in a way that was totally unnecessary, perhaps destroying it before it had a chance to grow. And even if things continued to go smoothly, how long could she be happy with him as her boss, in a position of authority over everything she did at the office? No, they had to be equal in every area of their lives.

As Jennifer looked down at Joe's handsome face, drowsing now in a satisfied half-sleep, a near-smile on his lips, she realized they had been lucky to have come as far as they had.

This was the first time in her life she was truly happy in a relationship. She owed it to herself and to him to do everything she could to make it work.

And if that meant leaving Eton, she would do it.

As she looked at Joe, taking in each feature she had explored with her gaze and lips and touch, she felt he truly did love her, even if he couldn't say it. And once she told him of her decision, he would probably be pleased that she was doing all she could to make the relationship thrive. She half-wanted to wake him up and tell him right then and there—it would be nice to share the decision—but knew it would be better to wait until she could tell him something definite. That way, any concerns he had about her not being able to find a job would be meaningless.

By the time Jennifer arrived at work a bit later though, much of her initial enthusiasm had dissipated. Finding another job now would be as difficult as it would have been when she was planning to leave Civette, if she hadn't already had Joe's offer. Perhaps it would be even more difficult. Now she would have to say she had been at Eton only a very short time, and the inevitable question would be Why are you leaving? No matter what her answer was, it simply wouldn't sound great.

But she'd try, in any case.

The first two people she called weren't in. The third, Charlie Hennessy, an old friend from Civette who was now v.p.-store marketing at Revelle, was glad to hear from her, and politely discreet about not asking why she wanted to leave Eton.

"But listen, Jennifer," he said. "Instead of banging your head against the wall trying to get a decent job at one of really just a few companies, why don't you open your own?"

She laughed. "My own what?"

"Consulting firm, of course. Doing what you do now. Everybody's doing it these days, and most people are failing miserably at it. But a few are doing quite well—really coming out on top."

"Hmm. I read an article about that in *Women's Wear* just a few weeks ago. I don't know though. It's such a—" She stopped. She had been about to say "risk." But it suddenly occurred to her. What was the big risk? It was certainly something of a financial risk, and if she failed, the venture wouldn't look great on her resume, especially after such a short stint at Eton. But who was to say she would fail? And if she ever wanted to try being on her own, now was certainly the best time to try. It could be tremendously exciting instead of frightening. "You know what, Charlie? I think I'm going to do it."

"That's *great*, Jennifer. Listen. Who knows if it will work? Who knows if anything will these days? But if anyone can do it, it's you."

She smiled. "Thanks. I just hope . . . well, with the economy what it is—"

"With the economy what it is, a really good person can do fantastically well. Unfortunately for us wage slaves, companies know that it's often cheaper to go to an outside firm if they want something done quickly and well. And that's where you could really clean up." He laughed. "As I remember, your idea of the workday was around the clock even when you were a mere hireling. Listen, Jennifer, go to it. And I don't know what the problem is at Eton—"

"None, Charlie. It's just time for me to leave for personal reasons."

"Ah. Then all the better. Sign them up as your first client. Do what you've been doing for them as an independent contractor. They'll need you to, anyway, if you're leaving."

Jennifer smiled. "That's a wonderful idea, Charlie. Thank you so much. For everything."

"No sweat. Just do me a favor though."

"What's that?"

"Stay away from Revelle until *I* say I need you. I may be out on the breadline soon because of people

173

like you. I don't want it to come any sooner than it has to."

"Okay." She laughed. "I'll talk to you soon, and with good news, I hope."

Charlie Hennessy's idea was absolutely perfect. Opening her own consulting firm would give Jennifer an independence she had been ready for for years, yet she would be able to continue to help Joe get Eton back on its feet.

For the next few days Jennifer said nothing to Joe or anyone else as she worked out the details of her plan. Part of what made it exciting, she felt, was the plan's utter secrecy. When she revealed the news, it would be a fait accompli, one she would have taken care of in every respect. And in the meantime she wouldn't have to argue with discouraging words from Joe, her father, or anyone else. She would take care of it all.

When she was with Joe, keeping the news to herself was difficult but not impossible. It was different from when she was hiding the truth about Caroline. This time, when she finally broke the news to him, he would be happy for himself, for her, and for their relationship. And if he was disappointed that he'd lose her at Eton, well, for one thing he wouldn't really be losing her, and for another, she knew he cared more about her happiness than the company's success.

And Joe was extremely busy anyway. He had met with the board twice in one week. In the first meeting he had convinced them to drop the investigation, which they did after he had promised the entire matter had been taken care of. And in the second meet-

174

ing he had—miraculously, Jennifer felt—received their go-ahead on both new projects: the Ardence contest, which was to be expected, and the new cosmetics line, which amazed and pleased Jennifer. Joe had said that her presentation had bowled them over, and that *all* credit was due to her. She was happy she would be leaving Eton only after having performed such strong last acts. It would make things easier all around.

Arrangements went smoothly. The very first bank Jennifer consulted agreed to give her a loan. She could afford the price her lawyer wanted for incorporating into Preston Marketing, Inc., and the papers would be ready in a week. A printer friend gave her a good price on stationery and supplies. She ordered a filing cabinet and desk for a corner of her living room, her office until business really picked up, and she was filled with ideas. Now all she needed was clients.

Exactly a week after Jennifer had decided to go out on her own she was ready to tell Joe, and she invited him for dinner. The evening would be a celebration of sorts—of her new venture, of their relationship, of their faith in each other. She made a simple but delicious meal—chicken tarragon, sliced tomatoes with basil, and peasant bread—and put on a simple but pretty outfit, a cotton knit square-necked tank top, flowing cotton skirt, and sandals. The desk and filing cabinet had already arrived, and she had made them fit fairly nicely at the far end of the living room by the windows. With fresh flowers she had just bought, and the apartment as neat as it had ever been, it looked almost like an office she had seen in *New York* magazine, which its decorator had, in the opposite situation, been trying to decorate like a living room.

When the doorbell rang Jennifer took one last, pleased look at her "office," and then ran to the door.

Joe was smiling when she opened the door, and he stepped forward, kissed her lightly, and said, "Happy celebration—for whatever it is." He handed her a beautiful bouquet of lilacs and kissed her again. "Our anniversary?"

She smiled and shook her head. "Nope."

He raised a brow. "Well, I *know* you haven't gotten a raise." He searched her eyes, and then grew serious. "This would be very happy news to me, Jen, if it were true," he said softly. His gaze bore into hers. "Are you pregnant?" he asked quietly.

She smiled, then laughed, feeling wonderful. She had hardly let herself think about marriage and children with Joe, and though he wasn't proposing, he had said more than she would have hoped for from a man who resisted commitment as he did. "No," she answered, still smiling. "You know that couldn't be it."

He shrugged and smiled, and led her over to the steps of the living room. "Then tell me," he said.

"Uh-uh." She laughed. "I'm going to prolong this a little while. I've kept it a secret for days and I can wait a little longer. I want to pour us some drinks for a toast."

She poured two glasses of wine and brought them into the living room, and joined Joe on the couch.

He nodded toward the new desk. "I see you've got

176

some new things," he said. "Does that have something to do with it?"

She nodded eagerly. "Very much to do with it." She stared. "Can't you guess?"

"No, what?"

She raised her glass. "Okay. Here goes. To Preston Marketing, Incorporated. In fact, incorporated as of tomorrow."

Not a muscle on his face moved. "I don't understand," he said quietly. He was frozen, immobile, and then he put the glass down on the table and stared at Jennifer. "What are you talking about?"

She smiled. "Don't you see? Preston Marketing, Incorporated! I'm going into business for myself."

He shook his head, his features grim. "No, I *don't* understand, Jennifer," he said coldly. His voice was sharp and distant, almost cruel. "Are you telling me you're leaving me?"

"Not *you,* Joe. Eton." He said nothing. Jennifer felt suddenly as if she were talking to a stranger, to someone who didn't know her or love her, or even like her. "Gee," she said, shaking her head. "I'm sorry, Joe. Maybe I should have broken the news to you differently." She shrugged helplessly. "I just thought you'd be so happy I was doing this."

He stared at her. "And why would I be happy?" he asked, his voice still chilly and foreign.

She had made a mistake telling him in this manner. She could see that. Now, she was on the defensive, trying to convince him of the rightness of something he was already dead set against.

"Why?" he asked. "Fill me in. Have I missed something?" he asked sarcastically.

177

"Joe, come on," she said. "You don't have to turn into a complete stranger. An angry one at that."

"Maybe I *am* a stranger. Maybe you are. I just find it difficult to believe what I hear without wondering whether I know you at all. Maybe I don't."

She sighed. "You know that's not true," she said, trying to imagine their lovemaking, their whispered thoughts, their shared hopes. But somehow it all seemed like a dream all of a sudden, for she definitely hadn't done those things with the man sitting next to her. "Look," she began, "let's start over, okay? And I'll . . . you'll see it's good news if I tell it in the right way."

He gave her a withering stare. "Just tell it, for God's sake, backwards if you want. But tell me."

She sighed. "I—I had just thought that things would be better if we didn't work together." She tried to ignore his growing frown and went on. "You know, you had said yourself at one point that you would almost rather not see me than see me and not be able to . . . whatever. But that wasn't why I did it, Joe. I did it because I had thought . . ." Her voice trailed off. How could she say *I had thought it would make our relationship stronger,* when he was acting as if they were total strangers? She looked down at her hands, trying to think. When she looked back he was looking down, his jaw clenched in anger.

"Joe, I'm sorry I'm leaving Eton. But I don't really consider it leaving, because I can do what I always did," she said hopefully. He turned to look at her. "You don't even know what I'm going to do yet, so I don't see why you're angry. It's going to be my own consulting firm, and I'll be doing exactly what I've been doing for years—only for more than one company."

He shook his head. "More than one company, perhaps. But not for Eton."

Her heart raced. "What do you mean? Joe, I *need* you—Eton. I'm counting on Eton to be my first client."

"Then you'll have to count again," he said coldly.

She searched his eyes for the bright light of affection she had seen so often, for the soft gaze that caressed and the depth that spoke of love. But she met only unfeeling, ungiving pools of blue. "I don't think you understand," she said, her voice quavering. "This is my chance. I'm young and I don't have anyone to look after. I don't have any obligations. When else can I do something like this, Joe? This is my *chance.*"

He stood up. She rose quickly. She couldn't bear to look up at him at a time like this. "I don't think *you* understand," he said coldly. "I need you—needed you—at Eton. And you knew that."

She swallowed. "That's different," she said. "Don't you see? You've been at lots of companies, maybe not as president, but—"

"That's right," he cut in. "You know how much it meant." He sighed and looked into her eyes. "I don't think I know you as well as I had thought," he said quietly. He narrowed his eyes. "I don't think we know each other as well as we had thought." He paused. "I . . . wish you the best of luck, Jen. I'm sorry I can't be part of it." He turned away, and began walking to the door. When he reached it, he turned around. "I'll have Sherry send your personal

179

items here, all right? As long as you're leaving Eton, I'd rather you left as of now."

Before she could say a word, he had gone.

Jennifer sank into the cushions of the couch. She lay her head back and stared at the ceiling, wondering what, exactly, had happened. Joe. It was all over. One moment he had been happy, loving, the Joe she had known. And the next . . . But perhaps she hadn't ever really known him. For the Joe she had known would never have acted as he had tonight, never have looked at her with those ice-blue eyes that shut her out completely. But what about the Joe she had made love to night after night, the Joe who had wrapped his arms around her and made her feel warm and safe and wonderful just by being there with his tender touch? What about the Joe who had seemed to love her, who had so happily proclaimed that they were "officially" together as if the issue had really been on his mind? He had been so easy, at times. So loving.

And he was gone.

ELEVEN

Jennifer didn't hear from Joe after that night. According to Sherry, who called Jennifer the very next day and almost every day afterward, Joe was in a foul mood all the time, snapping at anyone and everyone. He had told Jennifer's department and the rest of the company that Jennifer's decision to open her own consulting firm had been "sudden," and had left everyone to speculate in whatever manner they chose. He had also told Jennifer—through Sherry—that he would prefer it if she were not in contact with her assistants.

Caroline called Jennifer every day, as she had been doing since she had gotten the news she could stay on at Eton. And she consistently harangued Jennifer with the same questions: "Why don't you two get back together?" "What's the big deal if you don't work for Eton?" "Why can't I talk to Joe about it?"

Jennifer appreciated Caroline's interest and good

will, but she could discuss the problem with no one. She had been deeply hurt, and to tell of the joys only after they were over forever would be more painful than she was willing to stand.

As days passed Jennifer managed to find other clients. Charlie Hennessy changed his mind and asked her—"just this once"—for a marketing plan for a new line of lipsticks. Two small, up-and-coming cosmetics firms in Long Island City had jumped at her offer, and she had appointments with both next week. She was writing an article on jobs in the cosmetics industry for *Glamour,* and she had met an independent art director who was interested in teaming up with her on presentations. She knew she wouldn't have made the effort to get these jobs if she had been able to work for Eton, so in a sense Joe's turndown had been good for business. It had galvanized her into action, forced her to look at possibilities she would otherwise have ignored.

But she didn't really care. She went through her appointments with half her mind elsewhere, and was consistently surprised when she got what she wanted from the person she was seeing. She thought about Joe a lot, about the good times she had had with him rather than their sad parting—but most of the time she was simply elsewhere, closed off from the world and from herself.

She often thought of calling Joe, especially at times when she had talked with him in the past—late at night, during the eleven o'clock news, when they had phoned each other if they were apart, and before lunch, when they used to call each other. At those times they had kidded each other about who each was having lunch with, and whether the other person should be jealous. Memories of small episodes like these were the most painful, for she knew now that none of it had meant what she had thought.

And she knew, too, that if Joe had really loved her, and had just made a mistake that one night, he would have called by now.

In the trades she read good news of Eton's progress. Though *Cosmetics News* was silent on the subject of Eton, *The Wall Street Journal* and *Women's Wear Daily* carried frequent stories of Eton's new developments. The Amino-Actives line was due in the stores by mid-summer, and media plans were extensive, a reflection of Eton's "great confidence in the line," according to *Scents*.

Weeks passed. The summer grew hot, and Jennifer's work slacked off as clients packed up and went on vacation. Jennifer wasn't worried—she had made enough money in the first month, when she had worked almost around the clock, to last the rest of the summer. But she was lonely to a degree she wouldn't admit even to herself. She planned to continue working, go out to Long Island for a few weekends to try to unwind, and just forget the past as well as she could.

And then, one night, in the middle of the eleven o'clock news, Jennifer was dozing off in bed when a voice on television made her eyes fly open.

"Ardence." It was Joe's voice. Jennifer sat up and watched as a series of beautiful young women were shown walking, running, laughing, riding, sometimes with handsome men, sometimes alone. The settings were beautiful and varied, some wildly lush and others desert-stark. "You know you don't need a designer's name on your perfume," said Joe's voice. "You've got your own identity. You know you don't need someone else's fantasy; you've got your own. And we'd like to send you to the place of your dreams, anywhere in the world, for telling us your dreams. Anywhere. Where your dreams just might come true. Ardence. The scent, the life-style. Details at better drug and department stores everywhere."

Jennifer smiled, though there were tears in her eyes. *Where your dreams just might come true,* Joe had said. His voice had been so close, so warm. Now her only connection with him was through a stupid commercial. And her dreams had died.

The phone rang.

Jennifer jumped—the ringing was loud and jarring —and her heart pounded. For she knew . . .

"Hello?"

"How did you like it?" he asked.

She smiled. "It was pretty good. Nice voice, anyway."

"Mmm. Cut down on the costs, you know."

There was a silence. Jennifer closed her eyes against the tears that were welling up inside—tears of sadness, and anger, and incomprehension all coming to the surface. Joe's voice was as affectionate as ever, and it had released a flood of emotions she had pushed down below the surface for weeks.

"Jennifer," he said.

"What?" she said coldly. She wouldn't fall for it,

not for the warmth, the pull, the affection, not again, she wouldn't.

"I've thought of you con—"

"Don't," she interrupted. "Just don't. It's over."

He didn't say anything. Finally she heard him sigh. "I don't know how to begin," he said.

"Then don't. There's no point, Joe. It's finished. I don't want to see you, I don't even want to talk to you."

"Jennifer, please. I have to speak with you."

"I don't want to, Joe." Her voice was quavering. "Why can't you—"

"Are you alone?" he interrupted.

"What?"

"Are you alone, or do you have company?"

"I just heard you on TV, Joe. I'm hardly having a dinner party."

"Then I'm coming over," he said, and hung up.

Jennifer replaced the receiver and stared unseeingly at the TV screen for a moment. Joe was coming over; she'd be seeing him for the first time in weeks. And, oh, God, he sounded as he always had when she had loved him so much.

She jumped out of bed and ran into the bathroom to see how she looked. Her face was tear-stained and she rinsed and dried it quickly. And then she caught sight of the rest of herself, rather visible in a sheer lavender nightgown that brought out the gray of her eyes and made them almost violet. She could change, or put on a robe, but she decided to do neither. Tonight would be a night of no games, of total honesty. And Joe would remember her like this for the rest of his life.

Part of her protested that she was playing games, that she wanted to lure Joe as surely and easily as she knew she could. But she knew she wouldn't; the game was too dangerous.

The doorbell rang. Jennifer grabbed a robe and put it on as she walked to the door. It was over with Joe; he could remember her any way he wanted.

But when she saw him—in that first look before self-consciousness could set in with either of them, when he looked at her with eyes full of love and wonder and gladness—she knew only one thing: she still loved him.

He held out his arms and pulled her close, and buried his face in her hair as she gathered him against her.

"Oh, Jennifer," he murmured. "God. What a mistake we made."

She closed her eyes. She wanted to fight back, to block out his words. But she loved him. He was the man she had always loved.

When he drew his head back and she looked into his eyes, she remembered so deeply and painfully what it had been like to lose him that she was suddenly frightened. "I can't," she murmured. "I can't go through that again. I just . . . I want you here, but I want you to stay away."

He shook his head. "I can't do that. Jennifer, I . . . it's taken me a long time to realize what happened. I can hardly bear to think of that time, that last evening, the way I felt afterward." His eyes glistened with tears. "I was so furious when you left Eton. I felt it was a total betrayal, as if what we had

186

had meant nothing to you." He shook his head. "I had trusted you with everything. And you left."

"I left because I was trying to protect what we had, couldn't you see that?" Jennifer said. "Because I had to be independent."

"I know that now," he said, sighing. "I know it now, Jen. But for weeks, all this time"—he smiled—"I almost hated you for what you had done." He held her firmly around the waist, his hands molding the curve of her hips. "And at the same time I missed you so much I thought I would lose my mind."

"Why didn't you—" She shook her head. "Oh, Joe, it can't be this easy. I can ask why you didn't call, or you can tell me how you've changed, but it can't work."

He held her tightly. "Why not? Why can't it work? Jennifer, I love you." He smiled. "I said it, and it feels wonderful. Something I've never told any woman before because it was never true before." He shook his head. "You and I have been living under illusions, darling. We've both been told—by friends, by family, by society, even. We've never married because we're afraid to make a commitment. Maybe to some extent it was true. But, Jen, that was because I had never known anyone like you, never loved anyone like you."

He moved a hand behind her head and settled her cheek against his chest. "One thing I don't ever want to think about, Jen, is how I loved you and never told you. I realized—what if something happens to her, and she doesn't know?" He squeezed her tight. "God, how I love you. I was just so afraid of losing you I couldn't face what you wanted. I felt so alone all of a sudden."

She looked into his eyes, deep blue pools of love shining down at her. "I had thought I'd make you leave tonight," she said softly.

He shook his head. "I wouldn't have gone," he said quietly. "Not without telling you how I felt." He gazed into her eyes. "Jennifer, that night—that night you told me you loved me. Did you mean it?"

She smiled. "Of course I meant it." And then her smile faded. "But you didn't say anything, Joe. I felt I had made such a fool out of myself—"

"I was the fool—being so afraid. But it's not going to happen again, not ever." He paused. "Jen, when I thought you had good news, and that you might be pregnant, I had felt happier than ever before, I think. I want that for us—all of it." He hesitated. "And I know you have to be free, you have to be independent. We could arrange things in whatever way you wanted. But we'd be together, as a family—the two of us, and maybe more someday."

She smiled, her eyes shining into his. "You talked about dreams coming true tonight on TV," she said. "I think mine just has."

And he took her in his arms, and together they showed each other how beautifully they could make each other's most cherished dreams come true.

LOOK FOR NEXT MONTH'S
CANDLELIGHT ECSTASY ROMANCES ®

When You Want A Little More Than Romance—

Try A Candlelight Ecstasy!

Desert Hostage

Diane Dunaway

Behind her is England and her first innocent encounter with love. Before her is a mysterious land of forbidding majesty. Kidnapped, swept across the deserts of Araby, Juliette Barclay sees her past vanish in the endless, shifting sands. Desperate and defiant, she seeks escape only to find harrowing danger, to discover her one hope in the arms of her captor, the Shiek of El Abadan. Fearless and proud, he alone can tame her. She alone can possess his soul. Between them lies the secret that will bind her to him forever, a woman possessed, a slave of love.

A DELL BOOK 11963-4 $3.95

Seize The Dawn

by Vanessa Royall

For as long as she could remember, Elizabeth Rolfson knew that her destiny lay in America. She arrived in Chicago in 1885, the stunning heiress to a vast empire. As men of daring pressed westward, vying for the land, Elizabeth was swept into the savage struggle. Driven to learn the secret of her past, to find the one man who could still the restlessness of her heart, she would stand alone against the mighty to claim her proud birthright and grasp a dream of undying love.

A DELL BOOK   17788-X $3.50